# The Spook
# Who Sat
# by the Door

# African American Life Series

A complete listing of the books in this series can
be found online at wsupress.wayne.edu.

## Series Editor

Melba Joyce Boyd
Department of Africana Studies, Wayne State University

# The Spook
# Who Sat
# by the Door

A Novel by

Sam Greenlee

With an Introduction by
Natiki Hope Pressley

WAYNE STATE UNIVERSITY PRESS
DETROIT

Library of Congress Control Number: 2021950196

ISBN (paperback): 978-0-8143-4957-1
ISBN (e-book): 978-0-8143-4997-7

Cover design by Tracy Cox.

Wayne State University Press rests on Waawiyaataanong, also referred to as Detroit, the ancestral and contemporary homeland of the Three Fires Confederacy. These sovereign lands were granted by the Ojibwe, Odawa, Potawatomi, and Wyandot nations, in 1807, through the Treaty of Detroit. Wayne State University Press affirms Indigenous sovereignty and honors all tribes with a connection to Detroit. With our Native neighbors, the press works to advance educational equity and promote a better future for the earth and all people.

Wayne State University Press
Leonard N. Simons Building
4809 Woodward Avenue
Detroit, Michigan 48201-1309

Visit us online at wsupress.wayne.edu.

To my wife Nicky

# CONTENTS

# INTRODUCTION

## Natiki Hope Pressley

This book is about neither race nor politics, inequality nor revolt. Although race and politics are the backdrop, this book is about freedom!

Over fifty years ago, when my father, Sam Greenlee Jr., wrote *The Spook Who Sat by the Door*, some critics chose to see his book as simply an outlined plan to educate and train youth gang members in Chicago to violently overthrow the city. They overlooked the meticulous intentionality of *Spook*'s main character, Dan Freeman, a man on a mission to quench his thirst for freedom and justice.

Freeman lawfully infiltrated the CIA through an affirmative action recruitment program designed by a failing politician who sought to win back the "Black Vote." In an all-too-familiar political ploy, Dan successfully completed the program and gained field experience but was assigned to serve as the copy boy. He's kept in a nonthreatening position, void of authority and dignity. Dan's true motivation for joining the CIA was to use what he learned to empower his community and serve a purpose greater than upward mobility. The noted "Spook" performed menial duties, overcame ridicule, and endured blatant racism to work toward his ultimate goal—revolution.

There are those who would vilify Dan Freeman's character, calling him a troublemaker, rabble-rouser, an angry black man, a disgrace to our race, or just too aggressive and extreme. It is easy to see him as the antagonist in an American fairy tale, but I propose seeing Dan as a victim of two of America's greatest tragedies—inequality and injustice. Like many, Dan earned a merit-based promotion. He successfully completed the CIA training program, with all its rigor. He went from being a young man living in inner-city Chicago to a CIA agent, but because he's a black man, he would never earn the respect the position garners or experience the full benefits of his achievement. Dan determined it more expedient to use his access to the "system" as a weapon against it. Although his tactics in this book may seem overzealous and dangerous, the essence of his intent should not be ignored. Growing up black and poor in the inner city has a significant impact on societal perspective. The synthesis of pain and power drive Dan Freeman to extreme measures with unbridled passion. Honestly, when we look in the mirror, many of us can see parts of Dan glaring back.

The message is very clear for him: The fight against the system of racism requires an indirect approach, an impeccably designed covert operation. Freeman, the Spook, is a freedom fighter who deliberately puts himself in the center of every battle. "Spooking," as my family and I frame it, is just that—working from the inside out. Around the time of World War II, white soldiers often referred to their black counterparts as "Spooks," and, later, the term also referred to spies who were notorious for their ghostlike maneuvers. This double entendre represents the duplicity of Freeman's existence: a black man attempting to excel in a predominantly white career (on purpose), whose intention is to overthrow an entire city by establishing and training an inner-city youth guerrilla militia. This kind of duplicity is not unique to Dan Freeman—I believe all people of color in America adopt it, in some measure, to survive.

It is challenging to build successful families and careers while also being reminded constantly by politicians, judges, and police officers that your black life doesn't really matter. This is just one reason for the incredible frustration and unrest. Black and brown people in this country work hard to navigate and participate in a predominantly white society but also desperately seek a profound way to express and celebrate their own culture and heritage. It's a social merry-go-round, and the inconsistency is dizzying. This American experience is immensely disproportionate, riddled with injustice and hypocrisy that somehow survives from generation to generation.

The American experience of freedom has often been predicated on mandate, policy, or legislation—even the "freedom to choose" awaited legislation. The mere fact that freedom must be given implies that freedom is not intrinsic—we are not "born free." Our grade school educators taught us that freedom exists through a governmental act. Primary education delivered an early message that we were "free" to do whatever our teacher told us to do—follow instructions and leave only when the bell rings. There was no particular lesson on personal freedom or on the liberation of the mind and soul. Only lessons on physical freedom were worthy of attention.

Education is intended to prepare people to exercise the "freedom" to think and act independently. So why are we conditioned to relinquish our freedom in our formative years and then petition for it at the polls in our adult years? We are destined to remain slaves to a system of sociopolitical constructs that were cultivated in America. This is not to say that the systems of social and political oppression were born in America, but they are certainly nurtured here. Freedom, like hope and love, cannot be legislated but must be definitively qualified by demonstration—some external manifestation of its reality. For example, when someone says they love you, while you appreciate the confession, you await an action to validate that statement. There is a reason the phrase "random acts of kindness" was coined, and not "random confessions of kindness." To describe one as "kind" means that person has demonstrated kindness in their activities. In other words, freedom, like kindness, has limits. We measure our freedom by experience, not presumption. Words like *liberty, independence*, and *unrestrained* usually accompany *freedom*. Yet people without obvious restraints or who have a semblance of independence still eagerly pursue freedom. Why? I believe all people are created with an internal compass and a genuine desire for justice that guide them in the direction of true freedom. This book explores how Dan Freeman seeks out both.

When my father wrote this book, it was a shadow of his own life—a personal revolt against racial injustice, police brutality, and economic disenfranchisement. *Spook* is his termination letter to institutional racism and a clarion call for true liberty and justice for all. This was his valiant effort to encourage our heroes in the fight for social change and a willful discharge from the societal disease caused by the undeniable promotion of inequality and injustice in America.

I hope this book inspires every reader to evaluate what freedom looks like in their life and what they're willing to do to get it.

# The Spook
# Who Sat
# by the Door

# 1

Today the computers would tell Senator Gilbert Hennington about his impending campaign for re-election. The senator knew from experience that the computers did not lie.

He sat separated from his assembled staff by his massive, uncluttered desk, the Washington Monument framed by the window to his rear. They sat alert, competent, loyal and intelligent, with charts, graphs, clipboards and reports at the ready. The senator swept the group with a steely gaze, gave Belinda, his wife and chief aide, a bright smile of confidence, and said:

"All right, team, let's have a rundown, and don't try to sweeten the poison. We all know this will be the closest one yet: what I want to know is how close? Tom, kick it off."

"The campaign war chest is in excellent shape, chief: no major defectors."

"Good. I'll look over your detailed breakdown later. Dick?"

"I spent a week on Mad. Av. with both the PR boys and our ad agency. They both have good presentations ready for your approval, Senator. I think you'll be pleased."

"How do we shape up on TV, Dick? All our ducks in line?"

"Excellent, Senator. You'll be on network television a minimum of three times between now and election day—just about perfect, no danger of overexposure."

"Have you licked the makeup thing yet, Dick?" asked Belinda Hennington. "A small detail but it probably cost one man the presidency. We don't want that to happen to us."

"No sweat, Mrs. Hennington. Max Factor came out with a complete new line right after that fiasco. I think we'll be using 'Graying Temples,' in keeping with our maturity image. As we all know, the youth bit is out nowadays. Fortunately with the senator we can play it either way."

"Good show, Dick," said the senator. "Harry?"

"I've run the results of our polls through the computers, both the IBM 436 and the Remington Rand 1401. Louis Harris gave us a random pattern sampling with peer-group anchorage; Gallup a saturation vertical-syndrome personality study and NORC an ethnic and racial cross-section symbiology. The results check out on both computers, although I'm programing a third as a safety-valve check-out.

"The computers have you winning the election, Senator, but by less than three thousand votes. A small shift and there goes the ball game."

The senator, startled and troubled, glanced nervously toward his wife. She gave him a smile of reassurance.

"Do the computers indicate a possible break-through," he asked, "with any of the peer groups? How do we stand with the Jewish vote?"

"You're solid with the Jews, Senator. Where you're in trouble is with the Negroes."

"The Negroes!" exclaimed Senator Hennington. "Why, I have the best voting record on civil rights on Capitol Hill. Just last year I broke the ADA record for correct voting on civil rights with 97.64."

"Our polls reveal a sharp decline just after your speech requesting a moratorium on civil-rights demonstrations. If we can regain most of the lost Negro percentile, Senator, we're home free."

"No use crying about a lack of voter loyalty. This calls for a 'think session.' Perhaps we should have our special assistant on minorities and civil rights sit in; although I'm not sure how helpful he'll prove. Frankly, I'm disappointed by his performance so far."

"Judy," said the senator into his office intercom. "Think session in here. No calls, please, and cancel all morning appointments. And ask Carter Summerfield to join us, will you?"

The senator turned to his wife as they awaited the arrival of Summerfield.

"Belinda, I'm beginning to have serious doubts about Summerfield, he hasn't come up with a fresh idea since he joined us, and I don't expect anything other than tired clichés from him today."

"He's fine in a campaign, Gil, that's where he'll shine. I don't think you ought to rely on him for theory."

"Perhaps you're right. I guess it's not brains we're looking for in him anyway."

"No," she smiled. "That's his least valuable commodity to us."

The senator swiveled his leather-covered chair half-round and gazed out at the Washington Monument.

"This question of the Negro vote could be serious. I never thought I'd ever be in trouble with those people. We have to come up with something which will remind them I'm the best friend they have in Washington, and soon."

Carter Summerfield had sat in his office all morning, worried and concerned. He sensed the senator was not pleased with his performance and could not understand why. Summerfield had sought desperately to discover what it was the senator wanted to hear in order that he might say it, and was amazed to find that the senator seemed annoyed when his own comments were returned, only slightly paraphrased. In all his career as a professional Negro, Summerfield had never before encountered a white liberal who actually wanted an original opinion from a Negro concerning civil rights, for they all considered themselves experts on the subject. Summerfield found it impossible to believe Senator Hennington any different from the others.

He had spent the morning searching for the source of the senator's displeasure until his head ached; the handwriting was on the wall and Summerfield knew his job was at stake. He must discover the source of displeasure and remove it. Perhaps he should wear ready-made clothes? Had the senator somehow seen him driving the Lincoln, rather than the Ford he always drove to the office? It was essential never to have a more impressive car than one's boss. He told all his newly integrated Negro friends that. Had anyone discovered the encounter with the white girl in Colorado Springs when he had accompanied the senator on a trip to the Air Force Academy? He had been certain he had acted with the utmost secrecy and discretion. But he had known even then that it was a stupid move which might threaten his entire career.

Summerfield took two Gelusils and a tranquilizer and reached for the phone to inquire discreetly of his fellow integrated Negro friends if there was word on the grapevine of an opening for a man of his experience.

The phone rang. It was Senator Hennington's secretary summoning him to the senator's office for a think session.

Smiling, as always when in the presence of whites, Summerfield entered the senator's office, his eyes darting from face to face for some sign concerning his present status. But the looks of the other members of the staff were no longer funereal and the senator greeted him with a warm smile as he motioned Summerfield to an empty chair, briefly inquiring about his wife and children.

"It seems, Carter," said the senator, "that we're in serious trouble with the Negro vote." Summerfield frowned in sympathy and concern. "We must come up with a fresh, dramatic and headline-capturing act on my part which will prove to my colored constituents that I'm the best friend they have in Washington." He swept the room again with his steely gaze, Gary Cooper, back to the wall, but undaunted. "And we must do it today."

Summerfield nervously licked his lips. "How about calling a conference of the responsible Negro leaders to discuss your new civil-rights bill, Senator?"

The senator considered for a moment.

"I don't think so, Carter. To be perfectly frank, I don't think the bill will pass this session. White backlash."

"How about a fact-finding tour of the African countries?" said Dick.

"No, I did that last year and still haven't kicked the dysentery I picked up on safari in Tanganyika."

"How about a speech attacking apartheid at Capetown University?" asked Harry.

"I don't think South Africa would grant me a visa."

"Gil," said the senator's wife, "why don't we accuse the Central Intelligence Agency of a discriminatory hiring policy?"

"Segregation in CIA?"

"Yes. They have no Negro officers at all; mostly menial and clerical help."

"Are you certain, Belinda? This could be what we're looking for."

"I'm positive, but I'll check it out. We have a man in personnel over there, you know."

"Couldn't a charge of that nature prove counterproductive, Mrs. Hennington?" asked Dick. "CIA's almost as untouchable as the FBI."

"Not since U-2 and the Bay of Pigs. And this should prove an irresistible combination for the press: cloak and dagger and civil rights."

"I'm inclined to agree, Belinda," said the senator, who was usually inclined to agree with his attractive wife. "What's the best way of springing this thing for maximum impact?"

"Why not at the Senate Watchdog Committee hearings?" said Tom.

"But the hearings are closed," said the senator.

"It wouldn't be the first time we've used closed hearings for a press leak, Gil. I'll brief Mark Townsend over lunch here in the office on the day of the hearings," said Belinda.

"Excellent," said Dick. "A political columnist of his stature is perfect."

"Now, how do I play it in the hearings? Indignant, angry, or do I underplay?"

"Dignified, I think, Senator," said Harry. "You're shocked and saddened that the agency in closest grips with the forces of godless communism is shackled by the chains of racial prejudice."

"Right," said Tom. "You say that America must utilize the talents of its entire citizenry, regardless of race, color or creed, in the cold war."

"They'll deny it at first," said Belinda, "then probably claim their personnel files are classified, but they'll back down when they get enough negative press coverage. They're very image-conscious nowadays."

Carter Summerfield sat looking interested, but carefully silent. Advising the senator how to criticize other whites was definitely not one of his functions.

"I can program one of the computers to provide statistics showing the increased efficiency of the armed forces since their integration," said Tom.

"If CIA does select a Negro, he'll be the best-known spy since 007," said Harry.

"Well, he will find it a bit difficult after all the publicity he's going to get," said the senator.

"You mean, Gil," said his wife, "the publicity you're going to get."

The senator smiled.

"General," said Senator Hennington, addressing the director of the CIA, "it has come to my attention that there are no Negroes on an officer level in CIA. Would you care to comment on that?"

The other committee members looked at Senator Hennington with some shock. They knew he faced a close election in the fall, but this gambit was below the belt. The general, fighting to control his famous temper, replied icily.

"You know, of course, Senator, that our personnel files are highly classified."

"I'm aware of that, General, but this meeting is closed and we are all cleared for that kind of information."

"It's not true that we don't have any colored at the Agency. Our entire kitchen staff, our maintenance section and drivers are all colored."

"My question, General, concerned Negroes on an officer level."

"Well, we don't have any colored officers."

"Do you think, General, that a policy of racially selective recruiting which excludes a full 10 percent of our population is a wise one?"

"Yes. While I personally have no race prejudice, I feel Negroes are not yet ready for the highly specialized demands of intelligence work."

"Really?" said Senator Hennington, smiling a smile of patronizing pity into the face of bigotry.

"It's a question of sociology rather than prejudice; a gap simply exists between the races which is a product of social rather than racial factors."

"There are Negroes who have bridged that gap."

"If so, I would welcome them in CIA."

"I would suggest you make more of an effort to find them."

"Senator Hennington," said the committee chairman, in his rich, aristocratic southern drawl, "we all know that deceit, hypocrisy, duplicity are the everyday tools of our agents in the field. Much to their credit, the childlike nature of the colored mentality is ill-suited to the craft of intelligence and espionage."

"I'm afraid, Mr. Chairman," replied the senator, once again entering into the charade concerning race he had conducted with his southern friend for well over a decade, "I don't understand what you mean by 'the colored mentality.'"

"There is the question of cover," said the general. "An agent must be capable of fading into the background, adopting the guise of the person one cannot remember minutes after meeting him. Negroes in the field would be far too conspicuous."

"General, I'd rather not carry this conversation any further. I would appreciate a report in a month's time concerning the progress of the establishment of a merit-hiring policy at CIA."

The luncheon table had been trundled away and Belinda Hennington and the famous political columnist Mark Townsend sat in the conversation corner of the senator's office, sipping brandy from large snifters.

"Both the senator and I wanted to give you an exclusive on this, Mark," said Belinda.

"Thanks, Belinda. Are you sure this checks out? The government is supposed to be at the forefront in merit hiring."

"Not CIA. We're positive."

"I have a man at CIA—mind if I check him out on this?"

"Of course not; you can use 'an undisclosed CIA source' in your lead."

"This could bring civil rights back into the headlines. It's been suffering from overexposure lately."

"You're right, Mark. The public has tired of the same old thing: fire hoses, cattle prods, dogs on the one hand and singing, marching and praying on the other. Civil rights could use a good public-relations man."

"When will the senator make an official statement?"

"I should guess after the wire services and television pick up your beat. About three days, I should think."

"Sounds about right. Where will you conduct the press conference?"

"Right here. The Washington Monument makes a good backdrop for the television cameras; almost a Hennington trademark."

Townsend had left and Belinda was sipping a well-earned scotch-on-the-rocks when the senator returned. She mixed her husband a drink as he sank into the leather chair behind his big desk.

"How did it go today, dear?" she asked.

"Couldn't have gone better, honey. I'm certain this is it."

"Yes, dear, by this time next week we'll have the Negro vote wrapped up again." She handed the senator his drink and rested one sleek hip on the polished mahogany of the desk. "Never take the voters for granted. Even Negroes react eventually, you know."

"I'd have thought the CIA would have been more alert on a thing like this. If they'd had even one Negro officer, my charges would have fallen as flat as your sister's soufflés."

"If it hadn't been CIA, it would have been someone else. We're not likely to run out of institutions to accuse of segregation in our lifetime, darling."

They smiled at one another affectionately.

That November the senator won his reelection comfortably, the Negro vote accounting for more than his margin of victory.

# 2

Freeman watched the class reunion from a corner of the common room of the CIA training barracks. It was a black middle-class reunion. They were black bourgeoisie to a man, black nepotism personified. In addition to those who had recruited themselves upon receiving notice that the CIA was now interested in at least token integration, five were relatives or in-laws of civil-rights leaders, four others of Negro politicians. Only Freeman was not middle class, and the others knew it. Even had he not dressed as he did, not used the speech patterns and mannerisms of the Chicago ghetto slums, they would have known. His presence made them uneasy and insecure; they were members of the black elite, and a product of the ghetto streets did not belong among them.

They carefully ignored Freeman and it was as he wished; he had no more love for the black middle class than they for him. He watched them establishing the pecking order as he sat sipping a scotch highball. It was their first day in the training camp after months of exhaustive screening, testing, security checks. Of the hundreds considered, only the twenty-three present in the room had survived and been selected for preliminary training and, constantly reminded of it since they had reported, they pranced, posed and preened in mutual and self-admiration. To be a "Negro firster" was considered a big thing, but Freeman didn't think so.

"Man, you know how much this twelve-year-old scotch cost me in the commissary? Three bills and a little change! Chivhead Regal! As long as I can put my mouth around this kind of whiskey at that price, I'm in love with being a spy."

"You know they call CIA agents spooks? First time we'll ever get paid for that title."

"Man, the fringe benefits—they just don't stop coming in! Nothing to say of the base pay and stuff. We got it made."

"Say, baby, didn't we meet at the Penn Relays a couple of years ago? In that motel on the edge of Philly? You remember that chick you was with, Lurlean? Well, she's teaching school in Camden now and I get a little bit of that from time to time. Now, man, don't freeze on me. I'm married, too, and you know Lurlean don't give a damn. I'll tell her I saw you when we get out of here."

Where'd you go to school, man? Fisk? I went to Morris Brown. You frat? Q? You got a couple brothers here, those two cats over there. What you major in? What your father do? Your mother working, too? Where your wife go to school? What sorority? What kind of work you do before you made this scene? How much bread you make? Where's your home? What kind of car you got? How much you pay for that suit? You got your own pad, or you live in an apartment? Co-op apartment? Tell me that's the new thing nowadays. Clue me in. You got color TV? Component stereo, or console?

Drop those names: doctors I have known, lawyers, judges, businessmen, dentists, politicians, and Great Negro Leaders I have known. Drop those brand names: GE, Magnavox, Ford, GM, Chrysler, Zenith, Brooks Brothers, Florsheim. Johnny Walker, Chivas Regal, Jack Daniel's. Imported beer. DuPont carpeting, wall-to-wall. Wall-to-wall drags with split-level minds, remote-control color TV souls and credit-card hearts.

Play who-do-you-know and who-have-you-screwed. Blow your bourgeois blues, your nigger soul sold for a mess of materialistic pottage. You can't ever catch Charlie, but you can ape him and keep the gap widening between you and those other niggers. You have a ceiling on you and yours, your ambitions; but the others are in the basement and you will help Mr. Charlie keep them there. If they get out and move up to your level, then what will you have?

They eyed Freeman uneasily; he was an alien in this crowd. Somehow, he had escaped the basement. He had moved up to their level and he was a threat. He must be put in his place. He would not last, breeding told, but he should know that he was among his betters.

The tall, good-looking one with the curly black hair and light skin approached Freeman. He was from Howard and wore his clothes Howard-style, the cuffless pants stopping at his ankles. His tie was very skinny and the knot almost unnoticeable, his shoulder-padding nonexistent. He had known these arrogant, Chicago niggers like Freeman before, thinking they owned Howard's campus, moving in with their down-home ways, their Mississippi mannerisms, loud laughter, no manners, elbowing their way into the fraternities, trying to steal the women, making more noise than anyone else at the football games and rallies. One of those diddy-bop niggers from Chicago had almost stolen his present wife.

"Where you from, man? You don't seem to talk much."

"No, I don't."

"Don't what?"

"Don't talk much. I'm from Chicago."

"Chicago? Where you from before that? Wayback, Georgia, Snatch-back, Mississippi? You look like you just got off the train, man. Where's the paper bag with your sack of fried chicken?"

Freeman looked at him and sipped his drink.

"No, seriously, my man, where you from? Lot of boys here from the South; how come you got to pretend? I bet you don't even know where State Street and the Loop is. How you sneak into this group? This is supposed to be the cream, man. You sure you don't clean up around here?"

Freeman stood up slowly, still holding his drink. The tall one was standing very close to his armchair and had to step back when Freeman rose.

"Baby, I will kick your ass. Go away and leave me to hell alone."

The tall one opened his mouth to speak; a fraternity brother sidled up, took his arm and led him away. Freeman freshened his drink and sat down in front of the television set. After a lull, the black middle-class reunion resumed.

He had not made a mistake, he thought. All niggers looked alike to whites and he had thought it to his advantage to set himself apart from this group in a way that would make the whites overlook him until too late. They would automatically assume that the others—who looked and acted so much like their black representatives and spokesmen who appeared on the television panels, spoke in the halls of Congress, made the covers of *Time* and *Life* and ran the Negro newspapers and magazines, who formed the only link with the white world—would threaten to survive this test. Both the whites and these saddity niggers, Freeman thought, would ignore him until too late. And, he thought, Whitey will be more likely to ignore a nigger who approaches the stereotype than these others who think imitation the sincerest form of flattery.

He smiled when he thought about walking into his friend's dental office that day.

"Hey, Freebee, what's happening, baby? Ain't seen you in the Boulevard Lounge lately. Where you been hiding? Got something new on the string?"

"No, been working. Look, you know the cap you put on after I got hung up in the Iowa game? I want a new one. With an edge of gold around it."

"Gold? You must be kidding. And where you get that refugee from Robert Hall suit?"

"That's where I bought it. I'm going out to Washington for a final interview panel and I want to please the crackers." His friend nodded. He understood.

Freeman did not spend much time socializing with the rest of the Negro pioneers, those chosen to be the first to integrate a segregated institution. He felt none of the gratitude, awe, pride and arrogance of the Negro "firsts" and he did not think after the first few days that many of them would be around very long; and Freeman had come to stay.

They had calisthenics in the morning and then six hours of classes. Exams were scheduled for each Saturday morning. They were not allowed to leave the area, but there was a different movie screened each night in a plush, small theater. There was a small PX, a swimming pool, a bar and a soda fountain. There was a social area at each end of the building in which they lived that included pool tables, ping-pong, a television room with color TV, chess and checker sets. There was a small library, containing technical material related to their classes and light fiction, magazines and periodicals. There was a music room with a stereo console containing an AM-FM receiver and with records consisting mostly of show tunes from Broadway hits of the last decade. There were Coke machines. It was like a very plush bachelor officers' quarter.

There were basketball courts, badminton courts, a nine-hole golf course, squash courts, a gym, a 220-yard rubberized track, a touch-football field. After the intensive screening which they had undergone prior to their selection, none of the rest thought that the classes and examinations were anything more than window dressing. They settled down to enjoy their plush confinement during the training period after which they would be given offices in the vast building in Langley, Virginia, down by the river.

Freeman combined a program of calisthenics, weight training, isometrics, running and swimming, which never took more than an hour, usually less than half that time. He would watch television or read until dinner, take an hour's nap and then study until midnight.

No one at the training camp, white or colored, thought it strange that Freeman, a product of the Chicago ghetto, where Negroes spend more time, money and care in the selection of their wardrobe than even in Harlem, should be so badly dressed. Or that, although he had attended two first-rate educational institutions, he should speak with so limited a vocabulary, so pronounced an accent and such Uncle Tom humor. They put it down to the fact that he had been an athlete who had skated through college on his fame. Freeman did not worry about the whites because he was being exactly what they wished. The Negroes of the class would be ashamed of him, yet flattered by the contrast; but there might be a shrewd one among them.

There was only one. He approached Freeman several times with penetrating questions. The fraternity thing put him off.

"You a fraternity man, Freeman?" he asked once over lunch.

"Naw. I was once because of the chicks. You had to have that pin, you know. Almost as good as a letter in football. But I thought that kinda stuff was silly. I used to be a Kappa."

He looked at Freeman coldly. "I'm still a Kappa," he said. He finished lunch and never spoke to Freeman again.

Midway through the fourth week, three of the group were cut. They were called into the front office and informed that their grades were not up to standard, and that same evening they were gone. Panic hit the group and there were several conferences concerning what should be done. Several long-distance phone calls were made, three to politicians, five to civil-rights bureaucrats. The group was informed that they were on their own and that after the time, energy, money and effort that had gone into their integration, they should feel obligated to perform up to the highest standards. Freeman had received the best grades in each of the exams, but no one was concerned with that fact.

Two others left the following weekend, although their grades were among the highest in the group. Freeman guessed correctly that it was for homosexuality and became convinced that in addition to being bugged for sound, the rooms were monitored by closed-circuit TV. He was right. The telephones, even the ones in the booths with coin boxes, were bugged as well. The general received a weekly report regarding the progress of the group. It appeared that those intellectually qualified could be cut on physical grounds. They were already lagging at the increasing demands of the morning calisthenics and were not likely to survive the rigors of hand-to-hand combat. The director of the school confidently predicted that not one of the Negroes would survive the ten weeks of the school, which would then be completely free for a new group of recruits presently going through preliminary screening. It was to the credit of Freeman's unobtrusive demeanor that the school's director did not even think of him, in spite of his excellent grades and physical condition, when making his report to the general. If he had, he might have qualified his report somewhat.

The general instructed his school's director to forward complete reports to the full senatorial committee. He intended to head off any possible criticism from Senator Hennington. He could not know that the senator was not in the least concerned with the success or failure of the Negro pioneers to integrate the Central Intelligence Agency. He had won his election and for another six years he was safe.

"When this group is finished, I want you to begin screening another. Don't bother to select Negroes who are obviously not competent; they have already demonstrated their inability to close the cultural gap and no one is in a position seriously to challenge our insistence not to lower standards for anyone. It will cost us a bit to flunk out six or eight a year, but we needn't worry about harassment on this race thing again in the future if we do. It's a sound investment," said the general. He was pleased and again convinced that he was not personally prejudiced. Social and scientific facts were social and scientific facts. He ate a pleasant meal in his club that evening and noted that there were both white and colored present. The whites were members and guests; the Negroes served them. The general did not reflect that this was the proper order of things. He seldom approved of the rising of the sun, either.

Two more were cut for poor marksmanship. Freeman had obtained an ROTC commission at college and had served in Korea during the police action. He was familiar with all of the weapons except the foreign ones, and a weapon is a weapon. Only the extremely high cyclic rate of the Schmeisser machine pistol bothered him and that did not last very long.

"Mr. Freeman," the retired marine gunnery sergeant said, "that is an automatic weapon and designed to be fired in bursts. Why are you firing it single-shot?"

"It's to get its rhythm, Sergeant. I couldn't control the length of the bursts at first and I was wasting ammo, but I think I have it now."

The sergeant knew that Freeman had been an infantryman, and marines, in spite of what they claim, have at least a modicum of respect for any fighting man. "OK, Mr. Freeman. Show me what you mean. Targets one through five, and use only one clip."

"Call the bursts, Sergeant."

"Three. Five. Five . . ." He called the number of rounds he wanted in rapid succession, as fast as Freeman could fire them. There were rounds left for the final target and, on inspection, they found that one five-round burst had been six instead.

"That is very good shooting, Mr. Freeman. Were you a machine gunner in Korea?"

"No. I was in a heavy weapons company for a while and got to know MGs fairly well, but I spent most of my time in a line infantry company. I like automatic weapons, though. I learned it's not marksmanship but firepower that wins a fire fight. I want to know as much as I can about these things."

"All right, Mr. Freeman, I'll teach you what I know. You can have all the extra practice and ammo you want. Just let me know a day ahead of time and I'll set it up. We'll leave the Schmeisser for a while and start with the simpler jobs, and then work up. Pistols, too?"

"Yes, I'd like that, Sergeant. And I'd rather your maintenance section didn't clean them for me. I'd rather do it myself. No better way I know of to learn a weapon than to break it down, clean and reassemble it."

The gunnery sergeant nodded his head and something rather like a smile crossed his face.

Freeman read everything in the library on gunnery, demolition, subversion, sabotage and terrorism. He continued to head the class in examination results. There was much more study among the group now and they eyed one another uneasily, wondering who would be the next to go. They had no taste for returning to the jobs they had left: civil-rights bureaucracies, social welfare agencies, selling insurance, heading a playground in the ghetto, teaching school—all of the grinding little jobs open to a nonprofessional, middle-class Negro with a college degree. Long after Freeman retired, between midnight and one, his program not varying from the schedule he had established during the first week, the rest of the class studied far into the night. The group was given the army physical aptitude test, consisting of squat jumps, push-ups, pull-ups, sit-ups and a 300-yard run.

Freeman headed the group with a score of 482 out of a possible 500. The men finishing second and third to him in academics were released when they scored less than 300 points. There were only two other athletes in the group, one a former star end at Florida A and M, the other a sprinter from Texas Southern. They were far down on the list academically, although they studied each night until dawn. It was just a matter of time before they left. In two months there were five of the group left, including Freeman. Hand-to-hand combat rid them of two more.

The instructor was a Korean named Soo, but Calhoun, his supervisor, was an American from North Carolina. The niggers would leave or Calhoun would break their necks. He broke no necks, but he did break one man's leg and dislocated another's shoulder. He was surprised and angered to find that Freeman had studied both judo and jujitsu and had a brown belt in the former and a blue stripe in the latter. He would throw Freeman with all the fury and strength he could muster; each time Freeman took the fall expertly. He dismissed the rest of the class one day and asked Freeman to remain.

"Freeman, I'm going to be honest with you. I don't think your people belong in our outfit. I don't have anything against the rest of the group; I just don't think they belong. But you I don't like."

"Well, I guess that's your hang-up."

"I don't like your goddamn phony humility and I don't like your style. This is a team for men, not for misplaced cottonpickers. I'm going to give you a chance. You just walk up to the head office and resign and that will be it. Otherwise, we fight until you do. And you will not leave this room until I have whipped you and you walk out of here, or crawl out of here, or are carried out of here and resign. Do I make myself clear?"

"Yes, whitey, you make yourself clear. But you ain't running me nowhere. You're not man enough for that." Freeman felt the adrenalin begin coursing through his body and he began to get that limp, drowsy feeling, his mouth turning dry. I can't back away from this one, he thought.

"Mr. Soo will referee. International judo rules. No chops, kicks or hand blows. Falls and chokeholds only. After a fall, you get three minutes' rest and we fight again and I keep throwing you, Freeman, until you walk out of this outfit for good."

"Mr. Soo?"

They bowed formally and circled one another, each reaching gingerly for handholds on the other's jacket. He had fifteen pounds on Freeman and wore a black belt; but a black belt signifies only that the wearer has studied judo techniques enough to instruct others. The highest degree for actual combat is the brown belt Freeman wore. Calhoun was not a natural athlete and had learned his technique through relentless and painstaking practice. His balance was not impressive and he compensated with a wide stance. Freeman figured his edge in speed all but nullified his weight disadvantage. He had studied Calhoun throughout the courses; he had watched him when he demonstrated throws and when he fought exhibition performances with Soo. Freeman was familiar with his technique and habits and knew that he favored two throws above all others, a hip throw and a shoulder throw, both right-handed.

He came immediately to the attack. Freeman avoided him easily, feeling him out, testing his strength. Calhoun was very strong in the shoulders and arms, but as slow as Freeman had anticipated. He compensated by bulling his opponent and keeping him on the defensive.

Calhoun tried a foot sweep to Freeman's left calf, a feint, then immediately swung full around for the right-handed hip throw. Freeman moved to his right to avoid the sweep, as the North Carolinian had wanted, then, when Calhoun swung into position for the hip throw, his back to Freeman, Freeman simply placed his hand on his back and, before he could be pulled off balance and onto the fulcrum of Calhoun's hip, pushed hard with his left hand, breaking contact. It had been a simple and effective defensive move, requiring speed and expert timing. They circled and regained their handholds on each other's jackets. After a few minutes of fighting, realizing that he was outsped, Calhoun began bulling Freeman in an effort to exhaust him.

Soo signaled the end of the first five-minute period. They would take a three-minute rest. By now, Freeman knew his opponent.

You'd be dangerous in an alley, thought Freeman, but you hung yourself up with judo. Karate, or jujitsu, maybe, to slow me down with the chops and kicks. But there is just no way you can throw me in judo, white boy. He wondered whether to fight, or to continue on the defense. He looked at Calhoun, squatting Japanese-style on the other side of the mat, the hatred and contempt naked on his face. No, he thought, even if I blow my scene, I got to kick this ofay's ass. When you grab me again, whitey, you are going to have two handfuls of 168 pounds of pure black hell. He took slow, deep breaths and waited for the three minutes to end.

Soo nodded to them, they strode to the center of the mat, bowed and reached for one another.

Freeman changed from the standard judo stance, with feet parallel, body squared away and facing the opponent, to a variation: right foot and hand advanced, identical to a southpaw boxing stance. It is an attacker's stance, the entire right side being exposed to attack and counter from the opponent. Freeman relied on speed, aggressiveness, natural reflexes and defensive ability to protect himself in the less defensive position. He wanted only one thing: to throw this white man. He moved immediately to the attack.

Freeman tried a foot sweep, his right foot to Calhoun's left, followed up with a leg throw, *osotogare*, then switched from right to left, turning his back completely to his opponent, whose rhythm he had timed, and threw him savagely with a right-handed hip throw.

Calhoun lay there and looked at Freeman in surprise. He got slowly to his feet, rearranging his judo jacket and retying his belt. Freeman did the same, then, facing him, he bowed as is the tradition. Calhoun remained erect, staring at Freeman coldly. Freeman maintained the position of the bow, hands on thighs, torso lowered from the hips.

"Calhoun-san. You a judoka. You will return bow of Freeman-san," hissed Soo. Reluctantly, Calhoun bowed. They returned to their places on the mat, squatting Japanese style, waiting for the three minutes to end. Freeman wondered if he could keep from killing this white man. No, he thought, he's not worth it and it would really blow the scene. But he does have an ass-kicking coming and he can't handle it. This cat can't believe a nigger can whip him. Well, he'll believe it when I'm through . . .

Soo signaled them to the center of the mat.

Freeman methodically chopped Calhoun down. He threw him with a right-foot sweep, a left-handed leg throw, another hip throw and finally a right-handed shoulder throw. Calhoun, exhausted by now, but refusing to quit, reacted too slowly and landed heavily on his right shoulder, dislocating it. Soo forced the shoulder back into the socket and the contest was finished. Saying nothing, they bowed formally and Freeman walked slowly to the locker room. It was the end of the day, Friday, and he would have the weekend to recuperate. He would need it.

Calhoun asked for an overseas assignment. Within three days he left for leave at his family home in North Carolina, then disappeared into the Middle East.

Freeman would have to be more careful; there were holes in his mask. He would have to repair them.

# 3

The director of the school reported to the general on the new group.

"General, I'm afraid that there is at least one who might stick it."

"I thought you told me only two weeks ago that there was hardly a chance that any of that group would last."

"That's correct, General. Even with the facts on paper before me as I made the report, I somehow forgot that the man existed. He has a way of fading into the background. You can't remember his face, or what he looks like, or what he has said, even minutes after you have spoken to him. But the records speak for themselves. He leads the class in everything and his marks are above average, although not by much, for our regular classes."

"Who is the man?"

"His name is Freeman, sir."

"Is that the one who had the altercation with Calhoun?"

"Yes sir, and Soo reports that he could have killed Calhoun. Soo thinks him one of the finest natural judoists of his experience."

"But Calhoun is rated one of the best men we have in hand-to-hand combat."

"That's true, General; but in all honesty to Calhoun, this man has had several years' experience as a judoist. He has fought in the Midwest regional championships for the last three years, qualifying for the national finals, but refusing the trip because of work commitments. Our physical instructor considers him one of the finest natural athletes he has ever seen."

"True, they do make good athletes. Great animal grace and reflexes. I'm disappointed, however, in Calhoun. He should never have lost his head, challenged the man. Soo indicates that there was no provocation. He's just too dedicated to the agency. Can't stand the idea of standards being lowered. Can't say that I disagree with him. Well, he has a chance to prove himself in Yemen." The general picked up some papers from his desk in dismissal.

When the director of the school had almost reached the door, the general lifted his head. "This man Freeman, if he survives this group, is to go into the incoming class. He might do well among his own people, but competing with whites might be another cup of tea. He is not to be treated unfairly, but he is not to be given any advantage, either." The general motioned the director back to the chair. "What kind of man would you say he is?"

"Well, slow-witted, a plodder. He studies five hours a day, seven days a week. Only in athletics does he seem to do things naturally. Physically, he could be expected to react instantly and efficiently, but in a mental crisis, I don't know."

"I thought as much. Then there is no question of his going into the field. Even if he does survive the group, we cannot subject the lives of other agents in the field to his deficiencies. We will find something for him here in headquarters. Thank you, that will be all. Keep me posted on this group."

Two weeks before the scheduled ending of the training, Freeman was alone. He watched the last of the group leave. No one bothered to say goodbye; Freeman had no friends among them and his continued presence in the camp was an insult. He settled himself in front of the television set and pressed the remote-control button and watched the white fantasy world in full color.

Freeman finished the course and was congratulated in a small ceremony in the director's office. There were to be three weeks before the new group arrived and he elected to remain in the camp, except for a few days leave. He drove to an all-Negro housing development just across the Anacostia River and applied for a one-bedroom apartment. He then drove to New York and checked into the Hotel Theresa in Harlem. He made the rounds of the Harlem bars the first evening, before heading downtown to the jazz joints. His Robert Hall suit and too-pointy shoes were in the hotel closet, his gold-edged tooth cap in a plastic container in the bathroom, a plain one replacing it. He wore black-rimmed glasses of plain glass, cordovan bluchers, a button-down shirt of English oxford and a dark sharkskin suit from J. Press.

He saw Thelonious Monk at the Five Spot, the band with Johnny Griffin, Charlie Mingus at the Village Gate. He saw *Threepenny Opera* in the Village and *Five-Finger Exercise*, *The Night of the Iguana*, and *I Can Get It for You Wholesale* on Broadway. He visited the newly opened Guggenheim and decided that Wright had goofed, but he enjoyed the Kandinskys. He visited the galleries on Fifty-seventh Street and the Museum of Modern Art. His second night, he found a six-foot, compatible whore who knew the night clerk at his hotel. He tipped the night clerk and the bellboy on duty, and each night after that, he would meet her in the bar between two and three and they would spend the night in his hotel room.

He purchased sixteen books, but deferred delivery until further notice. The CIA Freeman would not have read those books.

Freeman left his suit, shoes, shirt, tie and tooth cap in a bag, with instructions that they be delivered to the storage company that stored the rest of his clothing, records, books and paintings that had no business in his new existence. He would establish a New York base later. He had pondered the danger of leading a double life and decided that the strain of squaredom would have to be eased somehow from time to time. The few days in New York, doing the simple things he had done, had convinced him more than ever that this was important. He might be the CIA Tom in Washington, but for a few days elsewhere he would have to become Freeman again. He did not think that, even if he ran into his CIA colleagues in New York, identification would be a danger; niggers all look alike to whites, anyway, and no one would connect the New York Freeman with the Freeman who would pioneer integration in one of the most powerful governmental institutions in the United States.

He left early Sunday morning, the top of the car down; he put the Morgan onto the New Jersey Turnpike and headed south for the nation's capital. The Morgan would have to go, he decided. It did not fit his painstakingly created image. He was sorry about that as he listened to the exhaust note over the roar of the wind and the car radio, but a Ford or Chevrolet would be better; perhaps even an Oldsmobile or a Buick. He would be expected to own a car a bit outside his means, a bit more

expensive and flashy than those of his peers at the agency. It was not difficult to conform to the image whites desired, since they did most of the
work. They saw in most Negroes exactly what they most wanted to see;
one need only impressionistically support the stereotype. Whites were
fools and one had constantly to fight in order not to underestimate their
power and danger, because a powerful and dangerous fool is not to be
underestimated. Add the elements of hypocrisy and fear and one had an
extremely volatile combination. It was a combination that could easily
blow the country, even the world, apart. In the army Freeman had learned
to respect but not fear the potential danger of explosives; rather, he had
learned how to use them.

He did not, as did the African diplomats, have difficulty with lunch on
Highway 1 because he did not bother to try to get a meal in the greasy
spoons and truck stops that dotted the highway like cancerous growths
of chrome and neon. He stopped along the highway and ate a lunch he
had packed the night before from a delicatessen. A premixed martini
over the rocks from a thermos, a cold chicken with potato salad, a mixed
salad with oil and vinegar dressing and a small bottle of Chablis, which
had chilled in the cracked ice of the cooler. Finished, he discarded the
ice, repacked the container and lay back on the army blanket he had
spread under a tree and slept for an hour. He reached Washington just
ahead of the incoming weekend traffic and was in camp in time to shower
and catch Ed Sullivan on television after a light dinner in the camp
dining room.

An agent, as Freeman had anticipated, had checked his movements
in New York, checking routinely at the hotel and questioning the whore
with whom Freeman had slept. They would not find much, since Freeman
knew that the people with whom he had talked would have seen nothing out of the ordinary in either his dress or behavior. Besides, Harlem
Negroes, particularly hotel employees and prostitutes, seldom tell white
men very much, especially those who look and act like cops, regardless
of what they claim to be.

Free of classes, Freeman increased his personal study and was able
to spend time each day working with Soo on the mat. He added karate to
his repertoire of judo and jujitsu and spent time as well on the range,

firing pistols, rifles and shotguns, as well as his more favored automatic weapons.

Freeman spent each weekend in Washington and became convinced that it is one of the squarest towns in the world. Within walking distance of the immaculate, white, neoclassical center lie some of the worst ghetto slums in the United States. The bigots on Capitol Hill need look no further than a few hundred yards to convince themselves of the inherent inferiority of Negroes and, controlling the capital like a colonial fiefdom, they can ensure that things will not change racially.

He found a whore on U Street and would spend time with her each weekend, in a bed in a hotel in the ghetto. She was questioned as well.

"Look, honey, what kinda cop you say you were?"

"I'm not a police officer."

"You look like a cop to me, baby. How come you asking me stuff about this cat? He in trouble? He a nice John. What make you think I'm going to tell you anything?"

"I'm not a policeman, but I do have police friends . . ."

"Like that, huh? I wondered when you start leaning on me. You ofays never no different, no matter how you look. And you college cats with the smiles and pink baby faces the worst. OK, what you want to know?"

He slipped her a twenty. She picked it up from the table, never taking her eyes off his face.

"Have you ever known him to take dope? Marijuana? Heroin?"

"Naw, he don't even smoke much. After he eats, after we done turned a trick, maybe three or four cigarettes all the time we together. He ain't no junkie, baby."

"Does he have a tendency to boast, brag?"

"Him? Naw, he don't talk about himself at all. I thought he was a baseball player, even football, although he a little bit small for that; but he could be, he ain't nothing but muscle and prick. If he got any fat on him, I ain't found it."

"Does he gamble?"

"Naw. One night I took him up to a place. Cat owed me some bread and I had to collect. Little poker, little craps. He just watch and when we through we leave.

"Tell you something 'bout that man, though. People don't give him no shit. He move quiet, don't say nothing, but I seen some bad cats move around him. This cat owed me the bread. He don't want to pay it. I don't tell him nothing about—what you say his name, Freeman? I don't say nothing about him being my man. I just took him there before we make it to the hotel and maybe he want some action, I get a cut. The cat owed me start to get a little off the wall about the bread, then he look at Freeman. He just standing there watching the crap game, quiet, ain't bothering nobody, but this cat owes me the bread look at him and then look at me and, baby, he give me the bread. And that cat one of the baddest men in D.C. He make two of Freeman, but he don't want no part of him. He ain't my man and it wasn't his scene, but I thought about it and if I had trouble that night, he be in it.

"And he ain't romantic about chicks on the block. Never comes on like a social worker: 'How a nice girl like you get into this shit.' 'Let me take you out of it, baby.' None of that shit. I'm a whore and he knows it, but he treats me like a queen. I think he putting me on for a long time and then I get to like it. He can put me on as long as he wants. I dig the way he treats me. I'm a whore. He knows it, I know it, but when I'm with him, he makes me feel like a queen."

"What about his sexual habits? Anything, well, unusual?"

She looked at him through narrowed eyes. "So that your scene? Well, baby, twenty bills ain't enough for no freaks. Come again. Little more bread, dig? I know some chicks don't deal in nothing but freakish tricks, but that ain't my scene. And don't start no shit about the Man. I ain't on junk and I can always get my hat and make it to Baltimore, dig?"

He gave her another twenty, blushed furiously and damned the woman for sensing what no one else knew, that he enjoyed this part of his job, to his shame.

"Nothing fancy, little straight up and down, mostly. Blow jobs ain't his scene. He don't mind a little head now and then, but before the deal goes down, he wants to make it straight. No way-out positions or jazz, whips and wet towels, no gimmicks. He just like to screw, baby.

"Now, don't be disappointed. Now, I could tell you 'bout some real freaks. I got a trick, white boy like you, come down here once a week, just to listen. Get his cookies every time. You want to hear some scenes, honey? Or maybe you want me to get a show together. Straight, gay, or both. Anything you want, baby."

They were sitting in the back booth of a long, narrow and very dark bar on U Street, She stroked his thigh and confirmed his excitement. This was the easiest trick she had in a week. She wondered how much she could milk him for.

"Would you say that he might have homosexual tendencies?"

She threw her pretty black head back and laughed. "Him? Man, you wasting your time there. He wouldn't make that scene for nothing. If you got a thing for him, look someplace else. Shit, I ought to know what I'm talking about, I make it that way myself and it takes one to know one.

"Anybody could turn me straight, it could be him. I mean, he don't need no fake scenes and he just want a good, professional job; but sometimes he really turns me on and I ain't had no thing for a man in years. No, baby, he ain't gay.

"But, if that your scene, I know somebody you might dig." She continued to stroke his thigh. "Or, baby, I could do things for you."

She leaned over, whispering in his ear and told him in detail what she could do. He backed into the corner of the booth, but continued to listen. Suddenly, he gripped her thigh with one hand and groaned. She moved away, looked at him in contempt, and then she lit a cigarette. He lay back against the corner of the booth until the color returned to his face, a thin film of perspiration on it. She crossed her legs and moved her foot in time to Sonny Stitt on the jukebox. She liked this joint; they had good sounds here.

He sat up and wiped his face with a handkerchief, looking around nervously. No one was paying the slightest attention to the booth.

She motioned toward the back of the bar. "The john back there." He started to slide across the bench of the booth.

"You forgetting something, honey." She held out her hand. He reached quickly into his pocket and stuffed crumpled bills into her hand. She looked at them, nodded and moved from the booth to let him pass. She smoothed her red dress, thinking that his grip on her thigh might leave a bruise. She walked to the bar and ordered a drink, fixed her hair in the mirror and straightened her red dress on her shoulders.

She had never worn red before, she had been told all her life that she could not, because she was too black, but Freeman had told her that she should wear it because she was a Dahomey queen.

She had gone to the library to find out what he had meant because he wouldn't explain, and asked for the book he had written down for her. She had found that he was talking about Africa and at first had been angry. But there was the picture of a woman in the book that had looked enough like herself to startle her, hair kinky and short-cropped, with big earrings in her ears. She had taken the book out of the library and painfully read it in its entirety. Then she bought a red dress and, later, several others when she found the tricks liked it, but mostly because Freeman liked her in red and said so. She wore big round and oval earrings like the queen in the picture, but she could not bring herself to wear her hair short and kinky; but sometimes she would look at the picture and see herself there and for the first time in her life, she began to think that she might be beautiful, as he said.

She returned to the booth and sipped her new drink. The trick returned from the john, all police-like and white-man strong. He thanked her for her information and cautioned her not to say anything to Freeman. He could not look her in the eye. She blew smoke into his face and he left. She would need no more tricks that night and she had done better than for a full weekend with the paddy-boy.

She walked to the phone booth and called her chick.

"Honey, got a scene working. I won't be able to make it tonight, big bread. See you tomorrow, huh?

"Of course I miss you. Be cool, baby. Mama will make it up tomorrow. Bye, now."

She walked out into U Street and took a cab to a small efficiency apartment that she kept for herself. Even her woman did not know of its existence and she used it when she wanted to be alone. She wanted to be alone tonight and to think about Freeman. She might invite him to her apartment the coming weekend instead of making their usual hotel routine. Men were not her scene, she knew, but she liked that man. She knew soon after she entered the apartment that she would invite him there.

# 4

**E**ach morning Freeman would drive his secondhand Corvair to the big building, descend three levels, unlock the door of his office and begin work. He ate in the cafeteria just often enough not to appear aloof; the rest of the time he would bring his own lunch in his briefcase and eat in his windowless room, listening to rhythm and blues or jazz from the Negro radio station in Washington on a transistor radio. He was the top secret reproduction section chief and, being the only man in the section, he was little more than the highest-paid reproduction clerk in Washington. Nevertheless, he was the only Negro officer in CIA.

He was promoted after a year in his cubbyhole. He had been making a run of two hundred of a three-page report dealing with the methods of bribery of Central American union leaders when there was a knock on the door. He stopped the Ditto machine, wiped his ink-stained hands on a piece of waste and opened the door to the general's secretary, Doris, a tall, golden girl from California with big breasts she considered a gift from the gods.

"Dan, the general needs someone to give a senator a guided tour of the building. Do you think you can handle it? I usually do it, or one of the other secretaries, but we're up to our ears getting ready for the closed budget hearings next week. Now, if you don't think you can do it, say so and I'll try to get someone else."

"I think I can handle it."

"Good, then, we can go right up to the general's office." She was standing very close to Freeman and when she turned she allowed one of her jutting breasts to brush his arm. She sat on the edge of his desk while he washed his hands in a basin in the corner.

"Don't you like me?"

"Why do you ask that?" he said.

"Well, you don't seem very friendly when you bring top secret documents up to the office. Sometimes you don't even seem to know that I'm around." She pouted prettily.

"Well," said Freeman carefully, "it's just that I have a great deal on my mind, the responsibility of running the entire top secret reproduction, you know. I want to make good and sometimes I'm preoccupied with my duties. You know how it is. Actually, I think you're very intelligent and attractive. Everyone says so. To be the general's executive secretary at your age is quite an accomplishment; all of the other brass have secretaries who are much older. I'll try not to be so preoccupied the next time I bring some things to your office."

He put on his coat and held the door open for her and she brushed him again as she passed. He turned out the light and checked the door carefully to see that it was locked. They walked to the elevator and he pressed the button to summon it.

"You're very ambitious, aren't you?" she said.

"Yes, I want to be the best reproduction section chief they've had here."

"Oh, but you are. Everyone says what a good job you're doing; much better than anyone ever expected. You know, I'm ambitious, too. I don't want to be a secretary all my life. I've applied for lateral entry into the officers' corps and if I pass the oral exams next year, I'll get an overseas assignment."

"I'm sure you'll pass." The elevator arrived and they entered it. He pressed the button for the top floor of the building.

"Well, I hope so," she said. "I'll probably start out under embassy cover, you know, handling cryptography and administration, but I hope eventually to be an operative agent."

"Well, I'm certain you'll be the prettiest spy wherever they assign you." They left the elevator, Doris managing to brush him again, and walked to the double doors of the general's suite of offices. They entered and Doris settled herself behind her desk in the outer office and waved to the door behind.

"Go right in, Dan. The general's expecting you." She thrust her breasts against the powder-blue cashmere sweater she was wearing and was smiling to herself when Freeman walked to the door of the general's office. He knocked on the door and entered.

The general waved him to a chair next to his massive desk. "Sit down, Freeman. Been hearing good things about you. Like being with our team?"

"Yes sir."

"Good. I think you know the building and the agency pretty well. Think you could take a group on a guided tour? As you know, we don't give many tours around here and are not staffed up like some of the other publicity-hound agencies. It's the Senate committee, or most of them, and we try to keep them happy if we can. Think you're up to it?"

"Yes sir."

"Good, then. Report to Morgan."

It was a group of three senators and three congressmen. The senator to whom Freeman owed his job was among them. Senator Hennington was pleasantly surprised to find Freeman his guide. He knew that the rest of the group had flunked out, but as long as there was one Negro, the CIA was integrated. The senator considered it another victory in his long battle in the field of civil rights. He was pleased to be faced with the fruit of his efforts.

"This, gentlemen, is our communications center, the nerve center of the agency. It operates around the clock, receiving and sending messages, from and to the far reaches of the earth. If the communications for one day were laid end to end, they would reach to Denver and back again to Washington.

"The center, of course, operates around the clock and is fully protected down here from anything except a pinpoint, direct hit of an H-bomb of at least one hundred megatons. The entire city of Washington could be destroyed and our communications center would continue to operate, carrying out its vital task as watchdog of the Communist conspiracy.

"In the next room is our computer system, capable of turning the raw material of intelligence, coming in through the communications center, into viable facts; the kind of facts that keep us at least one step ahead of the Reds. That one crucial step ahead, gentlemen, has probably meant peace until now for the free world. Lose it by even half, and we may well lose our freedom with it."

Freeman showed them through the building, climaxing the tour with a demonstration in the indoor firing range, himself firing alongside the regular firing master.

"That was certainly fine shooting, Freeman. Had you done a great deal of shooting before you came into the agency?"

"No sir, but the agency demands that we all qualify at least as marksman and a very high percentage check out as experts."

"That's very interesting. Tell me, where did you go to school? Howard? Fisk?"

"No sir. Michigan State and the University of Chicago."

"Really? They have some fine football teams at Michigan State. I'll never forget their Rose Bowl victory a few years back. Tremendous comeback in the last quarter. Were you out there for that one?"

"Yes sir."

"Senator, Freeman played on that Rose Bowl team," said Morgan.

"Is that right? You know, I played football for Dartmouth a few years back." He turned to Morgan, CIA congressional liaison officer, and asked: "Mr. Morgan, do you suppose Mr. Freeman could join us for lunch?"

"Of course, Senator."

They completed the tour and had lunch in the executive dining-room, the senator insisting that Freeman sit next to him. The senator was deft in handling Negroes. As he often told members of his own staff, it was important to make them feel comfortable, to treat them as equals. This was very difficult for the senator, since he really did not feel that there were very many people equal to himself, white or black. The senator had a polished, practiced humility that wore well, however. His wit, charm and good looks more often than not left people feeling that he was a regular guy; and although the senator did not feel himself a regular guy, he would have been pleased at the accolade, since Americans regularly elected "regular guys" to office.

"Tell me, Mr. Freeman, do you like working for the agency?" The senator had found that calling Negroes "Mr." often had a magical effect on the relationship.

"Oh, yes sir. I think it's an extremely important job and I'm proud to be a small part of the team."

"What were you doing before you joined the agency?"

"I was in social work in Chicago. I worked with street gangs in the slums."

"That's very interesting, Mr. Freeman. Did you enjoy the work?"

"Yes sir." Freeman used "sir" with whites as often as possible. He found that it had a magical effect on the relationship.

"Well, I think that kind of work is important. As I said in a speech on the Senate floor last year in our hearings on juvenile delinquency, it is extremely important that we establish some human and sympathetic contact with juvenile delinquents, school dropouts and other youthful members of the culturally deprived."

"I couldn't agree more, Senator."

"Yes. I favor a national study on the problem of juvenile delinquency and crime, particularly among the culturally deprived."

"Excellent idea, Senator. We certainly need another study of that problem."

"Then, of course, an increase in the construction of low-cost public housing, a training program for high-school dropouts and the introduction of scientific methods of rehabilitation in our reform schools.

"I'll send you a copy of the speech, Mr. Freeman. Unfortunately, the program was not adopted, but I have high hopes of some federal action in this area in the not too distant future. I was discussing this very thing with the president at luncheon just a couple of weeks ago."

"Yes sir."

"Did you find an increase of dope addiction among juveniles during your work with them?"

"Yes, Senator, I did."

"Yes, that is a major problem. We must strengthen our laws in that area. Make the penalties stiffer; but I definitely favor regarding the addict as a sick person, rather than a criminal."

"I couldn't agree more, sir."

"And, of course, there is the problem of increased illegitimate pregnancies among the youth of the culturally deprived. I certainly don't take the extreme stand of those who advocate sterilization, but advice concerning birth-control devices should certainly be made available and in some cases, they should be provided. Dependent on the individual case, of course, and tightly controlled."

"Definitely, Senator."

"There is a great deal of work to be done in this area. We have to roll up our sleeves and get to work. I told the president that last week and he agreed emphatically. I expect great progress in this area within the next few years."

The luncheon ended and the congressional party spent a few minutes in the office of the director. The senator lingered when the party began to leave for Capitol Hill.

"General, I was extremely impressed with Freeman. An excellent choice, I think. I had an interesting and enlightening conversation with him concerning his former field, juvenile delinquency. He gave me some excellent tips; things I might be able to use eventually in a Senate speech, or perhaps in an article for the *New Republic*. I think that taking him on as your assistant was an extremely wise move. It's fine to see integration in action."

Freeman was appointed the next week as special assistant to the director. He was given a glass-enclosed office in the director's suite. His job was to be black and conspicuous as the integrated Negro of the Central Intelligence Agency of the United States of America. As long as he was there, one of an officer corps of thousands, no one could accuse the CIA of not being integrated.

Freeman couldn't have been in a better position for what he intended to accomplish. He had access to most of the general's briefings, attended many of his meetings. He traveled with the general increasingly and his face became familiar throughout the agency. He took target practice three times a week, practiced judo, jujitsu and karate and had one weekly session of boxing with a retired former middleweight contender.

His routine seldom varied and the periodic checks by the security section confirmed this. He continued his trips to New York. He would check into the Hotel Theresa in Harlem, then leave for his apartment, shaking any possible tail. A shower, a shave, a Beefeater martini, and Freeman the Tom became Freeman the hipster.

No one ever blew Freeman's cover. They accepted at face value what he appeared to be, because he became what they wanted him to be. Working for the agency, in the agency, Freeman was the best undercover man the CIA had.

# 5

Freeman saw his Dahomey queen at least once a week. She told him of the interview with the agent, but he did not want to switch whores and complicate things: finding a mistress among black Washington society promised to be tedious, unrewarding, and a potential threat to his carefully worked-out cover. His girl, Joy, came to Washington almost monthly and twice she met him in New York midtown hotels, since he would not reveal his soul hole even to her.

Late one spring evening they were lying in his bed in Washington. They had eaten a seafood dinner in a restaurant not far from his apartment, just north of the junction of the Anacostia and Potomac rivers; they had been seated by the kitchen as usual. Later they had listened to Sonny Stitt in a small jazz club just off U Street in the heart of the big Washington ghetto. They made love when they returned but had not slept and lay silently sipping scotch and smoking, listening to the music of a late-night jazz station from the transistor radio which stood on the bed table.

Joy arose to one elbow and gazed into Freeman's face. "Dan, I think it's time to have a talk about the two of us. This kind of thing can't go on forever. It's time I started thinking about a home, family, security."

"OK," he said, "let's get married."

"Dan, you know I'd love to marry you, have your children, but this part of you, your bitterness, your preoccupation with the race thing—it frightens me, shuts me out. I feel threatened."

Freeman sat up in bed and looked at Joy in some surprise. "But why should you feel threatened? Hell, the way I feel doesn't even threaten whitey."

"Dan, how much longer are you going to stick with this job? You haven't had a promotion in four years and you're the only Negro officer they have."

"Once I prove myself, they'll recruit more Negroes; I'm certain of it. We can't all join the demonstrations; some of us have to try quietly to make integration work."

"Are you going to prove yourself by taking a bunch of bored house-wives on guided tours?"

They were on shaky ground and Freeman had to be careful; Joy knew him too well and one false move, a statement which didn't ring true, and he might expose himself. He arose, walked to the dresser to light a ciga-rette, regarding her in the mirror as he did so.

"I'm hoping I can move into something else soon; something more substantial." He returned to the bed, sat on its edge and lit a cigarette for her. "If I left now, before they began hiring other Negroes, I'd always think I'd given up. It's not easy continuing with this jive job, but it's little enough sacrifice for the cause of integration."

"Baby, I'm sorry, but I can't sacrifice my life for a cause. I admire the way you feel, but I fought too hard to get out of the slums and you continue to identify with the slum people you left behind."

"I never left them behind."

She placed her hand on his knee and smiled gently. "Honey, whether you admit it or not, the day you left Chicago for college, you left the block and the people on it. Besides, what's wrong with wanting to live in a decent neighborhood, to want the best for our kids?"

"Who do you think pays for those nice things if not the people we ought to be helping because nobody ever gave them a chance to help themselves? Joy, have you forgotten you came off those same streets? Except for your college degree, those people are just like you."

"Not me, baby! I left that behind me: all those hot, stinky rooms, those streets full of ghosts. Junkies, whores, pimps, con men. The crooked cops, the phony, fornicating preachers. And the smells: garbage, stale sweat, stale beer, reefers, wine and funk. That bad, hand-me-down meat from the white supermarket, the price hiked up and two minutes this side of turning a buzzard's stomach. I've had that shit and going back won't change things."

"Somebody has to try and change things."

"You can't change whitey. He needs things just the way they are, like a junkie needs shit. Whitey's hooked with messing with niggers and you want him to go cold turkey. It's not going to happen. We can be happy, Dan; we can be anything we want."

"Whitey won't let you be what you want to be, they put you in a pigeonhole marked nigger. How can I be happy that way? There's no way I can spin a middle-class cocoon thick enough for them not to penetrate any time they choose. Even if I could, what about the rest?"

"We have our own lives to live."

"I can't live in this country like an animal, I'm a man." He was restlessly pacing the room. She leaned toward him, the sheet falling away from her breasts, and he had a moment of panic looking at her, knowing that he might lose her.

"You don't have to live like an animal. If you really must spite whites, do it by succeeding. You can do more for your people by offering them an example to follow than by burying yourself in that building across the river."

"You mean hire myself out for a higher price to sit by a more impressive door?"

"It doesn't have to be that way; you don't have to think any cooperation with whites is a sellout. There are dozens of responsible positions available."

She wants me to tell her it will be all right if I make enough money. A man ought to be able to protect his woman, make her feel secure, but how long will it take for her to hate me as a man once I've traded in my balls? A showpiece spade is a showpiece spade, no matter how many times he gets his picture in the papers or how much bread he makes.

"Joy, I don't have to stay in Washington, I can return to Chicago." It was a bit soon for what he planned, but he had to try and keep her, keep them both. "There's an opening with the private foundation I started out with in street-gang work."

"You're going back into social work? All the good positions for Negroes are filled now. I thought you might finish law school, maybe go into politics."

She wants that title, he thought, Mrs. Lawyer Freeman, then Mrs. Congressman Freeman. "I can go to law school; the kids only hang out at night."

"Stop kidding yourself, Dan: you don't want to go to law school, you never did like it, and you hate Negro lawyers. You hate all the Negro middle class because you think they don't do enough to help other Negroes. You forget something, honey; I'm middle class, too, but you're still on the block in spirit. You've made your choice and I have a right to make mine."

He looked at her but she dropped her head and stared morosely at the glowing tip of her cigarette, its smoke lightly veiling her face.

"Yes," he said softly, "you have."

"I'm not coming to Washington anymore. I'm going to get married."

He picked up his drink and took a sip. The ice had melted and it was weak, watery and warm. "The doctor or the lawyer?"

"The doctor," she answered.

He drew a deep breath, let it out slowly.

"Seems like a nice cat." He thought of her never being his again and thrust the thought from his mind. He listened to the radio, Miles Davis playing a ballad. It didn't help; it was from a record Joy had given him as a present. How many other things had she given to him in their years together, how much of her was a part of him? Suddenly, he was afraid she would cry.

"I'm sorry, Dan, but I'm not getting any younger, and . . ."

"It's all right, baby," he said, taking her cigarette and snuffing it out in an ashtray. "I guess it had to happen one day. Look, this is our last night together; let's say goodbye right." He reached for her.

She sent him an invitation to the wedding and he sent them a wedding present, but he did not go to Chicago for the ceremony because he thought you could carry being civilized too far.


Freeman had met Joy years before in East Lansing, Michigan, when they were both students at Michigan State University. They were both slumbred, bright, quick and tough and considered a college degree the answer to undefined ambitions. They had much in common: they were both second-generation immigrants of refugee families from the Deep South. Their grandparents had migrated as displaced persons to the greater promises of the urban North: Joy's grandfather from Alabama to the Ford plant during the first war, Freeman's to the Chicago stockyards about the same time. Both Joy and Freeman had been born during the bleak depression years and had known the prying, arrogant social workers, the easily identifiable relief clothing, the relief beans, potatoes, rice and raisins wrapped in their forbidding brown paper bags. But poverty had done different things to them.

Joy had become determined she would never be poor again; Freeman that one day to be black and poor would no longer be synonymous. She regarded his militant idealism and total identification to his race first with amusement, then irritation and finally, growing concern. Joy had no intention of becoming her black brother's keeper. Slowly, she convinced Freeman he could best use his talents to help Negroes as a lawyer dedicated to the cause of civil rights. He could join the legal staff of one of the established civil-rights bureaucracies, to one day argue precedent-making cases before the Supreme Court.

She convinced him and he began preparing himself for law school while working toward an undergraduate degree in sociology. Life was being very kind to Joy; she had never felt she would marry the man she loved. But she knew she would have to be very careful because Freeman could be a very stubborn man and the mere idea of his becoming a member of the black bourgeoisie was enough to enrage him. Joy intended not only that he become a member, but one of the leaders. She felt that she could manage this essentially unmanageable man because he loved her. The greatest potential danger was that she loved him as well, but she thought that she could control that emotion. She would have to, because there was far too much at stake.

Joy made an unfortunate strategic error. She insisted that Freeman attend the national convention of the civil-rights organization they thought he would join. Because she had to work that summer to replenish her wardrobe for the fall, Freeman went to the convention alone. He returned bitter and disillusioned.

"Baby, there ain't no way I can work for those motherfuckers. They don't give a damn about any niggers except themselves and they don't really think of themselves as niggers.

"You ought to hear the way they talk about people like us. Like, white folks don't really have much to do with the scene. It's that lower-class niggers are too stupid, lazy, dirty and immoral. If they weren't around, all them dirty, conkheaded niggers with their African and down-home ways, why, everything would be swinging for the swinging black bourgeois bureaucrats, their high-yellow wives, their spoiled brat kids, and their white liberal mistresses. Integration, shit! Their definition of integration is to have their kids the only niggers in a white private school, their wives with a well-paying job in an otherwise all-white firm, and balling white chicks looking for some African kicks.

"And look at what they're trying to do. When did you ever see them raising hell with a lily-white union so that people like your father can get a job they're qualified for, or try to get those so-called building inspectors to do their jobs so people in the slums can live a little better, or get involved with any kind of nigger that wasn't just like themselves."

Joy was concerned, but not too much so; she figured that she could gradually smooth things over, but she underestimated Freeman's natural distrust and contempt for the Negro middle class; he remained adamant. Their fights about their future increased in frequency and intensity.

Freeman took frequent trips with the track team and it was not until he returned unexpectedly early from the annual Pacific Coast Conference-Big Ten dual meet, which had been held in Palo Alto, that he found that Joy had been spending each weekend he had been on the road with the track team, in Detroit. He drove to Detroit that evening, but she was not in when he called and he left a message with her mother. He called a former roommate who was doing graduate work at Wayne State and dropped his bags at his apartment. Freeman went to a little bar near his friend's home. He and Joy went there often because the bartender had been a potential All-American at Michigan until injured in the Army game and the owner of the bar had played football at Illinois. The bar had a small, tasteful combo; piano, bass, drums and electric guitar and sometimes a horn. He sat at the bar talking to the bartender, sipping a Ballantine's ale and listening to the music. He did not see Joy when she came in until he looked up and caught her reflection in the mirror behind the bar.

She was sitting in a booth almost directly behind where he sat and she had not noticed him there. She was with a tall, light-skinned Negro named

Frank, who had graduated from Michigan two years before. He was the Negro quota at a local medical school and his father was a prominent society doctor who made most of his money—tax free—selling dope to jazz musicians and performing abortions for Negro debutantes in Detroit.

Freeman watched them in the mirror and like lovers they touched one another in that way lovers think is casual. The bartender watched him closely and Freeman smiled that he intended to cool it. He was about to leave, hoping that Joy would not see him, when she looked up and their eyes met in the mirror. He nodded, smiled and lifted his drink in salute toward her reflection. He stood and walked to her table and talked small talk with her and her date. Freeman had met him often in Ann Arbor and East Lansing and occasionally at parties in Detroit, but somehow the pretty boy could never remember Freeman's name. Sitting there with Joy must have been good for his memory, because that night he knew exactly who Freeman was. They looked at one another in that quiet, deadly way men have when they don't like one another, while Joy chattered nervously. Freeman refused her invitation to sit down and then excused himself. He refused a drink at the bar and left, saying goodbye to his bartender friend.

To Frank's credit, he really wanted to marry Joy, but his mother would not permit it because Joy was not "society." She had not even "come out." Several days of his mother's illness, a round trip to Europe for the summer vacation and an American Express credit card convinced Frank that the thing between him and Joy could not work. He was very successful with the story of his tragic love in Europe and girls from Smith, Vassar and Sarah Lawrence sympathized with him right up until the time they climbed into bed with him. Somehow, the story did not impress the girls from Bennington. But the others were intrigued. They didn't know Negroes had problems of that kind. They would enclose his creamy body in their arms, shut their eyes and think of him as of the deepest black. Had he known this, he would not have been flattered.

The experience taught Joy a lesson. She would never leave her background behind her in Detroit; her beauty, grace, manners and education meant nothing to Detroit black society. She went to Los Angeles and became a society virgin from the Middle West. Freeman did not see her until years later, when she returned to Chicago.

# 6

The general became genuinely fond of Freeman, and while continuing to use him as a showpiece, began to use him increasingly as an administrative assistant as well. He seldom gave Freeman tasks more difficult than those he might award a reasonably intelligent secretary, but that he requested him to do more than mop the floor was in itself progress of no little degree. Even the most bigoted of the general's friends and colleagues gave him credit for "giving one of them an opportunity." It was as if the general had led the list in a drive for a popular charity. The general knew that Freeman would perform the tasks assigned him painstakingly, painfully and accurately. Freeman, in turn, learned the trick of making an easy job look difficult, a talent he shared with the vast majority of government employees in Washington, regardless of color.

The general began to take him on trips into the field more often, both at home and abroad. In the United States, of course, he would have his secretary inquire as to whether a Negro in their midst might offend anyone. Only a relative number of replies in the affirmative were received, confirming the general's pride in the progress of race relations. Freeman was often used as a liaison between the general and Senator Hennington and their mutual relations improved considerably. The senator would often invite Freeman to lunch in the Senate dining-room. The senator liked to lunch on the Hill with a Negro at least two or three times a month and often would be stuck with one who looked white, a wasted effort in image-making. Nowadays the presence of Negroes in the Senate dining-room seldom evoked any dramatic response from the southern senators, as had been the case early in the senator's career, thus taking much of the drama and pleasure from the adventure, but the senator's reputation as a flaming liberal crusader for human rights remained intact and Freeman made his small contribution, making only one minor faux pas by once requesting a wine in a good French accent. The senator did not notice and Freeman made a mental note that knowing anything at all about wines was not part of his image. The senator, flattered by Freeman's feigned ignorance and naïveté, told everyone that Freeman was an extremely intelligent man.

Freeman moved through Washington like an invisible man. He was an occasional, though not frequent, guest at Georgetown cocktail parties for African diplomats. He was seldom invited to sit-down dinners, not because the Georgetowners objected to eating with Negroes—they all did it several times a year—but to save him the embarrassment of which fork and spoon to use for which course.

His blackout from Washington black society, the most snob-ridden of a snob-ridden class in America, was total. It was as he wished. While Freeman could regard whites with a certain objectivity and controlled emotion, the black middle class and their mores sent him up the wall. He dated seldom and if there was a recurrence of the relationship, it was usually confined to bed. The Washington Negro women found much to fault Freeman in dress and cool, but little to complain about in bed. He seldom maintained a liaison more than a few months at a time. He still used the Dahomey queen, now moved up the whore's social ladder to the point where she was a high-priced call girl with a clientele consisting mainly of southern congressmen; she specialized in several sadistic variations, for which she charged extra. Her relationship with Freeman had become warm and personal, in spite of the fact that she knew nothing about him. She enjoyed his company, and increasingly she enjoyed sleeping with him. Men would never be her scene, but she knew by now that Freeman offered no threat and made no attempt to use the power her sexual enjoyment gave him. It intrigued her and she enjoyed the relationship they had.

Freeman studied the reports of the guerrilla fight in Algeria, particularly as confined to urban centers; the guerrilla war against the Huks in the Philippines; the guerrilla war against the Malayan Communists; the tactics of the Viet Cong; the theories of Giap and Mao Tse-tung.

He accompanied the general to Saigon four times as the war escalated. He stayed in the Hotel Caravelle, the air conditioning so high that you had to wear a jacket or a sweater. He had cocktails on the roof terrace among the correspondents who were trying to turn the day's ration of rumors, gossip and USIS and PIO propaganda into a meaningful dispatch. He ate in Vietnamese restaurants, several of the good French restaurants and a Japanese restaurant, set in a Japanese-designed garden, across town from the hotel. He learned to walk slowly the other way when a crowd surged toward the scene of carnage created by a terrorist, to watch if a cyclist had an egg more lethal than those laid by hens in the basket of his bike.

He bought a set of Danish-style stainless ware in Japan, a Japanese camera in Hong Kong, Thai silk in Bangkok. He had suits made by Jimmy Chen in Kowloon, which he had shipped to his New York apartment. He became adept with chopsticks and learned to make love in several languages. He found that in Asia he was not as hip in bed as he had imagined and took a postgraduate course in sex, oriental style. He was enjoying the job, its prerogatives and putting on so many white people, but the general saved him from any addiction in that direction.

They were driving back to Langley from the Capitol when the general decided to take his assistant to lunch. He almost requested that the driver stop at his club. Although the club had no colored members, it was no oddity to see dark faces there several times a year. Only recently there had been a Nobel Prize winner, an operatic star, a federal judge and the president of Howard University. But Freeman might be uncomfortable in the impressive surroundings of the club. The general ordered the driver to take them to a good, moderately priced steak house instead.

They were ushered in and taken to an excellent table. It was the first time in several visits that Freeman had not been seated by the toilet or kitchen. Freeman ordered a martini on the rocks, the general bourbon and branch water while they awaited their steaks.

"Dan, I want to say how pleased I am at the way you've fitted into the agency. To be frank, I had my reservations at first, but they've been completely eliminated by your performance. If more of your people were like you, there would be much less difficulty." The general took a sip of his drink, rolled it on his tongue a moment before swallowing, then made a tent of his fingers.

"Honest sweat and toil. Pull yourself up by the bootstraps like the immigrants. These demonstrations and sit-ins stir up needless emotion.

Your people must demonstrate a respect for law and order, earn the respect and affection of whites. Take yourself as an example: a fine natural athlete; no denying you people are great athletes."

"Yes," said Freeman, "and we can sing and dance, too."

"Right. In the fields of sports and entertainment, you're unsurpassed. But you must admit there's still a social and cultural gap to be closed. The Africans did develop centuries later than the Europeans, you know.

"As I've said, you're a fine athlete, but I think you'd have to admit your intellectual shortcomings. It will take generations, Dan. It's not a question of prejudice, but rather one of evolution."

Their steaks arrived and Freeman fought to keep his down. He had no appetite now and he willed his hands not to tremble. He had not ordered wine because he thought the spartan general might consider it an affectation. He sipped the cool Carlsberg, taking a deep breath as he replaced the glass. He forced himself to look at the general, masking his seething emotions. He surprised himself by summoning a smile.

"I'm encouraged after knowing you, Dan. You're a credit to your race. Perhaps your generation will achieve more by example than your civil-rights leaders can hope to accomplish through turmoil and agitation."

Somehow Freeman got through the meal. He excused himself as the general ate his dessert of apple pie à la mode and was violently ill in the toilet. He washed his face and saw how pale he had become in the washroom mirror, but he didn't think anyone as color-blind as the general would notice.

The general allowed Freeman to leave the office early that day and he reached his apartment ahead of rush-hour traffic. He mixed a stiff scotch and lay sipping it in a very hot tub while listening to Dinah Washington. Well into his second drink, he watched the six o'clock news: the big mounted cops charging the children with cattle prods, the police dogs and fire hoses, one long shot of a little girl bowled over by the battering stream of water and spun along in the gutter like a bowling pin, the freedom songs and praying, all the wasted, martyred faith and courage of a people who wouldn't quit. It had to be channeled where it would be most effective, where it might make whitey back off. It was time to stop procrastinating, time to do what he had to do; he had all the training he needed.

He walked into his bedroom, made a list of social welfare agencies in Chicago and wrote letters of inquiry concerning job openings. He discovered his hands had stopped trembling and that he was calmer than in years.

He requested an appointment with the general the next day. Freeman told him he had been profoundly impressed by the general's talk at lunch the day before. He felt he could make a greater contribution to his people by returning to Chicago and working among them and the general had shown him the way. The general reluctantly agreed that perhaps following his own advice might indeed be the best thing for Freeman to do. The general walked Freeman to the door of his office while heartily booming clichés concerning Freeman's grand sense of duty. He closed the door behind Freeman, frowned briefly, walked to his desk and phoned his director of training and personnel, informing him that they would need another Negro sometime within the next year.

He hung up and returned to the direction of the cold war.

# 7

F reeman left the director's office and walked directly to the elevator, nodding briefly at the director's secretary on the way out. He pressed the button calling the elevator to his floor and inspected the attaché case he had been presented as his going-away present. It was serviceably large, of saddle-stitched leather, with brass fittings. It contained the few things he had cleared from his desk in the office which had been his for years in the suite of offices behind the armed guards and door marked, simply, "Director."

The elevator arrived and he rode it down, walked across the vast marble hall to the entrance and waited at the door for the director's limousine. He had known that it would not be awaiting him at the steps and he showed no surprise, no anger. He had waited many years for what he had to do and a few minutes more for a car was no problem. It might take him many more years to do what he had planned for so long, and, an impatient man, he had carefully schooled himself in patience.

He stood at the door looking out into the huge courtyard of the building and out toward the trees that screened the building from the Potomac River, toward the city of Washington, hidden by the trees. The courtyard was bright with the Virginia spring sunshine, unveiled by factory fallout. He could not hear the birds behind the big glass doors of the entranceway, but he knew that they would be singing in the trees that lined the river. He had often brought his lunch to eat among the trees there, listening to the birds, watching the slow current of the river, sitting among the pines and sycamore, recalling the smells and sounds of summers spent in a boy-scout camp in Michigan. A city boy from Chicago, he had never lost his awe and love of the woods; their sights and sounds. The building squatted vast and ugly, a marble and granite conglomeration of the worst of neo-classical and government-modern architecture, an ugly abscess created by bulldozers and billions in the midst of the once-beautiful north Virginia woods. A cancerous abscess, he thought, sending out its tendrils of infection tens of thousands of miles.

He stepped through the door into the sunshine and listened to the sounds from the woods, placing the case at his feet. He was dressed in quiet bad taste, his suit a bit too light, his cuffs a bit too deep, lapels a bit too wide, shoulders a shade too padded, tie too broad, trousers too wide at the knee and ankle, socks too short. He wore large airplane-type sunglasses, his hair was closely cropped and there was a thin surrounding of gold around a front tooth. His suit was a bit too cheap and his wristwatch, of eighteen-carat gold, a bit too expensive. He walked with a gangling shuffle, his head tilted slightly toward one shoulder and there was always a smile on his face, even when alone in the building in which he worked, broadening and flashing the thin gold when people approached. He was very well liked and would be missed. Waiting for the director's car, he never once glanced back at the building in which he had spent a great part of the last five years of his life.

The black Cadillac limousine swung into the drive and stopped just ahead of where Freeman stood; the Negro chauffeur made no effort to get out to open the door. Freeman knew that he wouldn't open the door for him and patiently walked to the car, opened the door for himself and climbed into the air-conditioned interior. The driver started moving before Freeman was seated, throwing him awkwardly into the far corner of the rear seat. Smiling gently, Freeman disentangled himself and leaned back into the foam-rubber cushions, looking out at the Potomac River as they sped towards Washington, through the bulletproof glass.

"You really going through with it? You really quittin'?"

"Yes," said Freeman.

"And they ain't pushing you out. I thought so at first, but they ain't pushing you out. I didn't think cats like you ever quit a scene like you got. I seen a lot like you in Washington, but I never knew one to quit on his own. Your kind love it here. You don't even quit for more money someplace else. It just don't make sense. You really going back to that job you had, like they say? Working with street gangs in Chicago?"

"Yes, but this time I'll be in charge of the program."

"I shoulda known! A title, a goddamn title, the only damn thing you cats dig more than money. 'Special assistant to the director' wasn't enough; now you going to be a director yourself, or did they think up something more fancy?" The driver snorted in disgust.

Freeman said nothing and they proceeded along the riverside road in silence. They moved briefly through Arlington and then onto the drive and past the cemetery, the big statue of the marines raising the flag on their right. They went across the bridge and past the pompous Lincoln Memorial, the phallic Washington Monument at the end of the reflection pool, and just short of the next bridge, the Jefferson Memorial. The cherry trees were in bloom, a blaze of pink against the green, the blue sky above, with big, fat cumulus clouds floating marshmallowlike against the bright, blue sky. They turned right on Pennsylvania Avenue and drove to the White House where the guard waved the car into the drive.

In front of the White House, the driver again did not bother with the door and Freeman let himself out and walked into the Office Annex. He was met at the office door by a pudgy, red-faced man with nervous mannerisms.

"Dan, how are you? Right on time, right on time. We'll be going in to see the president in—" he looked at his watch and then glanced up at the clock on the wall behind the desk of the secretary "—exactly ten minutes. Now, we go in between the boy-scout delegation from East Bengal and just before his monthly tea with some of the congressmen's wives. Split-second timing around here, you know, and you know how he is if there is a foul-up. We have four minutes with him and then it's finished. He'll give you a little present, say a few words and then you pose for pictures. Should get some play in the Chicago press, which won't do you any harm and I'll send copies to you in Chicago next week. I don't know what his present will be; he's pretty cagey about that kind of thing, but you know what kind of response to give: little surprise, gratitude, thanks and tell him how sorry you are to be leaving the team. But I don't have to coach you, Dan. You know what to do, hey, boy?

"You know, we're all going to miss you around here. Remember that time he gave a rebel yell in the Taj Mahal and you smoothed things over with the Indian press? We haven't forgotten that, boy, around here, not a little bit. You were always in there swinging in the clutch. Yeah, sorry to see you go. Keep in touch now, you hear?

"Make yourself to home. I got to go check on those congressmen's wives. Be right back and then we can go on in."

Freeman sat in a big leather armchair and looked at the big four-color portrait of the president on the wood-paneled wall behind the secretary. In a few minutes the red-faced man returned.

"All right, let's go now. We stand outside his office until the boy scouts come out; then we go right in. You know the drill."

They waited at the door until the scouts left beaming, each holding a multipurpose jackknife. They entered the office of the president.

The president was seated in his rocking chair. His aide bent over and whispered in his ear as Freeman approached. The president arose and extended a hand, thrusting his own quickly far up toward Freeman's thumb so that it couldn't be squeezed, a trick learned from countless campaigns and handshakes.

"Well, Foreman, mighty glad to see you again. Sit down, sit down." He had heard Freeman's name incorrectly. The aide looked at Freeman in a moment of panic. Freeman ignored his misspoken name and the aide relaxed in gratitude.

"Well now, son, they tell me you're leaving us. Sure we can't get you to change your mind? The general, now, tells me he's mighty sorry to see you go. Says you do a good job over there by the river, and the general doesn't hand out praise very easy, you know."

"Yes sir, I know, and I'm flattered that he wants me to stay, but I'm afraid I have to leave. I've given it a great deal of thought and conscience calls. You see, I'll be going right back where I grew up to try and use my education to help kids who are like I used to be."

"Well, Foreman, that's a right fine attitude, but don't you think you might be making a bigger contribution for those very people here in Washington? Offer some inspiration for them to achieve, to emulate you? You know, local boy makes good."

"That's a point well taken, Mr. President, but I'd rather make my efforts in a more personal way: my small contribution to our Great Society."

"Well now, that's good! Very good! We could use you around here maybe speech writing. I like that: 'a small contribution to our Great Society.'" The president turned to his aide. "Put that down, Smitty; want to see it in my next speech." He squinted and gazed out into space. "As your president it is my humble pleasure to be able to make a small contribution to our Great Society. Got that, Smitty?

"We could use more of your idealism around here, Foreman. I certainly wish you the best of luck. I spoke to your mayor last week and they plan to do more in that area. I'm sure he could find room for you in his new commission."

"Well, Mr. President, I already have a position with a private social welfare agency, one I worked for before I came into the government."

"Well now, Foreman, never underestimate the good the government does for the people, even though I am a firm believer in private enterprise, as you know."

"Yes sir, I recognize the great contributions the government has made toward the lives of the individual citizen and that it is at the head of the war on poverty, but there have to be increased efforts by private agencies and individuals."

"You're right, of course. We can't have people dependent on the government to take care of all of their problems, now can we?"

"No sir, and I always ask not what my country can do for me, but what I can do for my country."

The president's smile tightened, his aide hastily thrust a package into his hand. "Foreman, here's a little memento I'd like to let you have, a little token of my appreciation of your efforts in your country's behalf."

Freeman opened the package. It was a multipurpose pocket knife, identical to those handed to the East Bengali boy scouts. Freeman wondered if the congressmen's wives would find pocket knives useful. He smiled his thanks.

"You remember that time we were on that tour of the East and all that fuss they made because I gave a little old rebel yell in the Taj Mahal? Well, you sure handled those Indian newsmen well. But I never could understand why they were so riled."

"Well, sir, it's a tomb, you know. It was a little like someone being disrespectful in the Alamo."

"Well, now that you put it that way. But I meant no disrespect."

"Yes sir, I told them that." His aide gave him a signal and the president rose and grasped Freeman's hand.

"Down my way, when you give a man a sharp instrument as a present, you have to give him something in return so that the friendship isn't broken."

"Yes sir. Here you are." Freeman slid off his tie clasp and gave it to the president. There was a cold silence, the president's grin frozen on his face. His aide hurried Freeman to the door.

Recovering, the president called out: "Now, if you get down my way, you stop in to see me, you hear?" The president frowned down at the tie clasp in his big hand. It was in the shape of a PT boat.

Freeman walked out into the bright spring sunshine, paused on the steps of the White House and looked out at the traffic on Pennsylvania Avenue. He walked to the side of the building to the parking lot. The chauffeur was leaning against the fender of the shiny black Cadillac, smoking a cigarette. He looked up at Freeman.

"Well, big-time, the Man say you can have the car as long as you want it today. Where you want to go?"

"You can go back to the office. I have a bag in the hotel where the airport limousine leaves for National. I'll walk from here."

The driver looked at Freeman and flipped the butt at him. It landed just short of the toe of his shoe. Freeman looked at the still-smoking cigarette butt, then he looked up at the driver.

"Nigger," he said, "if you had hit me with that butt, it would have been your black ass!"

The driver stiffened and moved forward from the fender of the car.

"Come on," said Freeman, "you been wanting some of me for years now. Let's get it on. I'll lay your black ass on the White House steps."

"You'd like that, wouldn't you? You out of a job and now you get big and bad in front of the White House. No, I ain't going to fight you here. You come down to U Street and I'll kill you."

"You couldn't kill me on the best day you ever had. Now you can drive me. Let's go!" The driver started around the hood of the car to the driver's seat. Freeman stood at the door and waited until he had reached the other side. "Nigger, open my door."

They stood looking at one another across the long, low top of the car, their elongated reflections almost touching. The driver walked slowly back around the car and opened the door. Freeman got into the back seat. He told him the name of the hotel where he had been staying since the packers had shipped his effects to his new apartment in Chicago the weekend before. They stopped at the entrance and Freeman passed the check for his bag to the driver. He got out, then returned with the bag without a word. They rode to National Airport in silence. When they arrived at the terminal, Freeman got out and handed the driver his plane ticket.

"Park the car and check my bag through. Bring the ticket to me in the bar upstairs." He walked into the terminal and upstairs to the bar and ordered a Carlsberg. He sipped the cold brew until the driver returned.

"Here's your ticket, big-time. One day I'm going to kill you."

"Go polish the car, boy. You won't be killing me anytime."

The driver stood looking at Freeman's reflection in the mirror to the rear of the bar. Freeman, sipping his beer, coolly returned his stare. The driver frowned in curiosity. He had never seen that expression in the five years Freeman had been with the agency. Finally he turned without another word and left the bar.

That was stupid, Freeman thought. Five years cooling it and when I blew it, it had to be him. Hell, we could probably be pool-shooting buddies, tasting a bit and chasing chicks. But there was no other way, the cover had to be complete, no holes anywhere. It had to be that way and now he was ready. Or was he? Had his mask become him? He would find out soon now. Had he really put them on, or had he been putting himself on for half a decade? Although trained for it, he had never been allowed to be a functioning agent; but then, that was not why he had been recruited. They had never felt he had either the guts or intelligence to function in the field and he had reinforced their thoughts on that score. He smiled to himself. He had conned them all and in his own way had been the best of the spooks and they might never know it. For five years he had been the CIA nigger and his job had been to sit by the door.

# 8

reeman was toward the head of the line waiting to board the Friday noon flight from New York to Chicago. He had closed his New York apartment, shipping those things to Chicago he chose to keep. He had listened to some jazz, attended several plays and shed his old cover as a snake sheds its skin. He boarded the plane and seated himself, moving with the grace and economy of a fit and well-trained athlete; gone the insecure shuffle, the protective, subservient smile, the ill-fitting clothes. The new Freeman, J. Pressed and Brooks button-downed, seated himself after placing his carry-on bag beneath the seat, fastened his seat belt and opened a little magazine with a psychedelic cover to an article urging the legalization of pot.

When aloft, he asked the stewardess if he might mix his own martini; he had once ordered a martini on a flight and found that the label proudly claimed a mixture of an eleven-to-one ratio. Freeman, particularly the new Freeman, was a four-to-one man, on-the-rocks with a lemon twist. By the time he had finished his drink and eaten the plastic lunch, the plane was beginning its descent to O'Hare Field.

He moved forward to the terminal gate and caught sight of his new boss. Freeman accepted his outthrust hand.

"Dan, how are you? Welcome back to Chicago; glad to have you aboard."

"Thanks, Mr. Stephens, it's good to be back."

"Dan," he smiled, with the air of a man bestowing a gift, "call me Steve." They moved down the wide tunnel with the crowd, toward the huge main hall of the terminal building.

"Right, Steve," Freeman smiled back.

"Did you receive that last batch of material I mailed you on the foundation and its work?"

"Yes, I thought the brochure superb."

"The best PR firm in Chicago did that; my old advertising connections come in handy. That brochure will prove invaluable in fund raising. Never underestimate the power of advertising, I always say.

"Any baggage to claim, Dan?"

"No, I only brought this bag with me. I shipped everything else ahead of me. It should be in my new apartment now."

"Fine. There's no need to stop in the office, we'll drop you at your apartment. Now, you take as long as you need settling in; no pressing need to report into the office before late next week."

"I'll be in Monday morning, Steve." They walked through the automatic doors to the exit and stood waiting at the curb. Stephens motioned to a Ford station wagon across the way. Imprinted on its front doors was the legend: South Side Youth Foundation.

"I remembered you and Perkins worked together years ago when you both worked for the mayor's youth commission, so I had him drive me down to pick you up." The car slid to a smooth stop in front of them and when they were seated, Freeman leaned over to shake the hand of the slim Negro seated behind the wheel.

"Perk, what's shakin', baby?"

"Hey, Dan; good to have you back." He moved the car smoothly into the outgoing traffic and south on Dan Ryan Parkway.

"Dan," said Stephens, withdrawing pipe and tobacco pouch, "you have your work cut out for you here, but since you're familiar with our operation, it should shorten the breaking-in period. Your first job in social welfare was with the foundation, wasn't it? Before I took over."

"Yeah, we worked out of a storefront on Fifty-third Street."

"We've come a long way since those days," said Stephens, proudly. "Our new quarters are worth more than a million and we've had several sizable grants since I took charge."

"How's the contact with the street gangs?"

"As well as could be expected, except for the Cobras."

"They won't let our street workers near them; call us 'whitey's flunkies,'" said Perkins.

"We're hoping your appointment might change the image, Dan."

Stephens toyed nervously with his unlit pipe. "A meaningful contact with the Cobras and we could get that Ford grant the next day."

"They were on a real Afro kick for a while," said Perkins. "We thought they might have some connection with one of the Afro-nationalist groups, but it doesn't seem so."

"But we can't discount that possibility; it's one of the things we'd like to know about the Cobras, Dan," said Stephens. They had moved through the hole cut for the expressway through the bowels of the main post office and now they were moving south again on the Outer Drive.

"They're potentially the most dangerous gang in Chicago," said Perkins.

"The Cobras will be my personal responsibility; I'd like their file to study over the weekend, Steve, if I may."

"Fine, Dan. I'll have Perkins deliver it to your apartment later this afternoon."

"Perk, I want to check out the Cobra turf tomorrow. Pick me up at my place at ten o'clock; Saturday night should be a good time."

"You know the Cobra turf, don't you, Dan?" asked Perkins.

"I ought to, I grew up over there. I was the Cobra warlord when I was a kid. They used to call me Turk."

"I never knew that, Dan," said Stephens.

"Yeah, the gang goes on. Street gangs and churches are about the only durable social institutions in the ghetto."

"You've certainly come a long way since your days as a Cobra, Dan," Stephens said proudly, as if personally responsible. They stopped in front of the pretentious entrance of Freeman's apartment building.

"I'll see you first thing Monday morning, Steve. I'll see you right after that, Perk, and I want a meeting with the street workers at three in the afternoon."

"Good to see you taking charge this way, Dan. How about lunch on Monday?"

"Fine, Steve, see you then." Freeman felt things had gone well and he anticipated no trouble from Stephens. He entered the building, took the elevator to his floor, entered his new apartment and began perfecting his new cover.

In less than a month the apartment said everything he wanted about the new Freeman. Cantilevered bookshelves covered the wall of one end of the living room. He drank and served Chivas Regal, Jack Daniel's black label, Beefeater gin, Rémy Martin, Carlsberg, Heineken, Labatt and Ballantine. He had matching AR speakers in teak cabinets, Garrard changer with Shure cartridge and a Fisher solid-state amp with seventy-five watts power per channel. A Tandberg stereo tape recorder, a color television set, which could be played through the stereo system, and videotape completed the system.

There was a Bokhara prayer rug on the plastic parquet floor, wall-to-wall nylon carpeting in the bedroom and wall-to-wall terry cloth in the bathroom. His glasses were of crystal, his beer mugs pewter, his salad bowl Dansk and his women phony.

He slipped on his cover like a tailored suit, adjusting here, taking in there until it was perfect and every part of him, except a part of his mind which would not be touched, was in it and of it. He found that most people did most of the work as far as his cover was concerned: they wanted him to be the white-type, uptight Negro of "rising aspirations" and desperate upward mobility. He chose his wardrobe with sober, expensive care, opened a number of charge accounts and slid into barely comfortable debt.

He fell into step with others like himself, safe, tame, ambitious Negroes, marking time to a distant drummer, the beat hypnotic, unsyncopated, the smiles fixed on their faces, heads held high to pretend the treadmill did not exist and that their frantic motion was progress. More white than whites; devout believers in the American dream because fugitives from the American nightmare. The yawning chasm of ghetto misery at their Brooks Brothers backs, they trod its edge warily, their panic hidden behind bright smiles and the sharpened wiles to tell the Boss Man what he wanted to hear.

Freeman attended dull cocktail parties, becoming a bachelor to invite, a prized escort. He was Playboy-suave, witty, well-dressed and never drunk or disorderly. He could talk *Time-Life-Newsweek* or Sunday *New York Times-Manchester Guardian-New Statesman* or little magazine-*New York Review of Books*. He could talk Antonioni, Truffaut,

Polanski, Hitchcock, New Wave; football, basketball, track and boxing. He had a way of making a comment and making it sound as if the listener had said it. He could flirt with the women without angering their men; make the fairies feel at ease and turn down their propositions without bruising their ego.

He ran into Joy in the bar of the Parkway ballroom and made a rendezvous for an afternoon the following week at his apartment. He told himself that he would not be there when she arrived, right up until the time she walked into his apartment, bronze, lovely, bewigged and smelling of Arpège.

She walked gracefully around the apartment, inspecting it minutely, stroking, feeling, touching while he mixed their drinks. He handed her her drink and she smiled catlike at him, taking a sip.

"Rob Roy. Honey, you never forget anything, do you? It's wonderful to have you back. The grapevine is saying all kinds of things about your new job."

"They wanted to slide me into the number two slot, prop up some white boy, but I wasn't having any."

"Whatever happened to dedicated Dan? I knew a time when position wouldn't have been as important as making a contribution. You've changed, honey."

"No reason why I can't make a contribution and make some money at the same time."

"How much is the job worth?"

"I'll be able to live on it."

"I used to be in the game, too, remember? I could make a pretty good guess. The poverty program really inflated salaries; everybody's getting more money in social welfare nowadays."

"Yeah, everybody but the poor."

"Next year the president will be handing out Washington appointments to buy the black vote and with that much time in your new job, you'll be in a good position for one. More money and in Washington where the cost of living is lower." She leaned forward for a light, watching him shrewdly over her cigarette.

"Maybe I shouldn't have been so impatient; I always knew you'd change, you like nice things as much as I do. We're really two of a kind, Dan. You're just more romantic about it than I am, and more idealistic. You always did get your nose open about slogans to save the world."

"Too late now, baby, you have a husband."

"After a fashion. His drinking is worse and he'd spend all his money on women if I let him. I don't care how many he has as long as he's cool with it and I have enough money to have whatever I want. His latest scene is a white girl on the North Side. And from Alabama, can you top that?"

"You had him followed?"

"Sure. I don't care what he does as long as I know it. We'll have to have you by sometime soon."

"No thanks. You know we never dug one another."

"Why should you be bugged? You know he never forgot we had a thing? He'd have a fit if he knew I was here." He listened to her chatter about her apartment, her hired help, her new car and wardrobe and thought she had come a long way from the girl from the Detroit slums he had known years ago in East Lansing. Her voice was polished, her mannerisms and gestures assured; she wore her expensive clothes with easy grace. She wore an expensive wig and he found himself wondering if she removed it when she made love. Later, he found that she did.


In order to confirm that the Cobras were the best organization for his plans, Freeman studied them carefully from a distance. He talked casually with anyone in the neighborhood willing to discuss the Cobras. He carefully built personal dossiers of each key gang member, in particular the gang leaders, Dean, Scott and Davis. He gradually worked out their chain of command and was pleased to find it efficient and effective. The rigid discipline of the gang impressed him more than anything else; discussion was permitted, even encouraged, but once a decision was made by one of the commanders, that decision stood. For most of the gang members, the Cobras provided the only family they had ever known, offering protection, affection, a sense of belonging, a refuge and haven from the unremitting hostility of the outside world.

Once certain of the Cobras, Freeman made his move. He casually walked into their poolroom headquarters not far from south State Street one cool evening. He walked to an empty table in the rear, selected a sixteen-ounce cue, rolled it on the table to test it for warp and began running balls. The owner of the poolroom walked the length of the room to Freeman's table.

"Look, mister," he said, "I think it might be better for you and for my place if you took one of the other tables."

"I like this one," said Freeman, without looking up from the table.

"This table is used by the leaders of the King Cobras." He waited expectantly. Freeman continued to run balls and did not answer. The man sighed and walked away shaking his head.

Freeman hadn't had a pool cue in his hands in years. He had spent much of his adolescence in poolrooms and it came back quickly, the easy stroke, wrist relaxed, the follow-through, English to leave the ball ready for the next shot. When he had run the balls, he tapped the butt of the cue on the floor and the owner walked to the table and racked the balls. He broke the varied colored pyramid, studied the table and began shooting bank.

He noticed the sudden silence in the room while studying a difficult shot. Without looking up, he shot, a bank shot twice the length of the table. Before the ball could drop into the left-hand corner pocket, a black hand intercepted it, held it a moment until Freeman looked up, then carefully replaced it on the green table.

Freeman looked at them across the length of the table, three Cobras staring at him silently. He returned the stare. The room was silent, no click and clatter of ivory ball against ivory ball, the chatter and banter of the players gone from the smoky room. They stood silent and dangerous, just beyond the light suspended above the table. Freeman chalked his cue, still staring at them, then lined up his next shot.

Freeman knew them, Do-Daddy Dean, the gang leader, Sugar Hips Scott, secretary-treasurer, and tall and deadly Stud Davis, the warlord and at nineteen oldest of the three.

"This our table." The voice came from the shadows, low, soft and dangerous.

"I want to talk with you."

"No talk, man, move out. No talk for social workers, man."

"You know who I am?"

"Yeah, we know who you are."

"Let's step outside and talk. It won't take long, just a few minutes."

"You don't want to talk, man; you just want to go home. Better that way. I don't ask no more, done asked too much already."

Freeman motioned to a door in the rear which opened onto an alley-way. "I'll wait for you out there." He walked out into the darkness and waited, facing the door.

They came out silently, spread out to arm's length and without pre-liminaries, moved in.

Freeman moved swiftly, crabwise in a circle to his left, bringing him-self closer to the man on his left and away from the other two. He stabbed toward his eyes with stiffened fingers and when he covered, Freeman gave him a stiff-fingered jab, elbow and wrist locked, his arm in close to his body, to his opponent's solar plexus. When he doubled, Freeman pushed him into the legs of the one in the middle and in one motion moved to meet Stud Davis. Davis feinted a left and crossed a right, catching Freeman high on the head. Freeman countered with a left and right, which Davis slipped, then he kicked Davis hard in the ankle. One of the others was rising, the one he had not hit, and Freeman whirled and gave him a judo chop just below the left ear, dropping him. He turned to Davis and threw him with a foot sweep to his good ankle. Freeman moved to the door of the poolroom, shut it, returned and sat on an upended Coke-bottle crate. When they stirred, he had them covered with a snub-nosed Smith & Wesson .38 revolver.

"Don't move. Just sit there and listen."

"Next time we see you, social worker, we have that, too."

"You ain't goin' to shoot nobody, small-time, and you sure as hell ain't goin' to shoot me. Now you shut up or I'll pistol-whip all the black off your ass.

"You think you bad, the King-ass Cobras. Nobody messes with you. You make Molotov cocktails and burn and loot supermarkets. Yeah, I know what you were doing on the West Side in July when they had the riots over there. Three supermarkets, a pawnshop, two furniture stores and a television store. That color TV in the poolroom came from there."

They stared at him in sullen silence.

"The big-time Cobras. Lifting cameras and small-time shit from pawnshops, sniping at cops with pistols and .22 rifles from rooftops. You know how much chance you have of hitting anything with weapons like that from that range at night? What the hell you trying to prove?" He looked at Stud Davis. "The fuzz wasted three snipers and wounded eight others and the only casualties they had was from getting hit by bricks and bottles. You're damn lucky they didn't hit any of the Cobras.

"OK, you want to hurt whitey, you want to mess with Mr. Charlie, then stop playing a bunch of punk games. You didn't do any more damage than a mosquito on an elephant's ass!" Freeman paused, he had their attention now. "You really want to fuck with whitey, I'll show you how!"

# 9

"**G**entlemen," Stephens said in a board meeting in his best advertising-executive manner, "I have splendid news." He paused dramatically, sweeping the room with his smiling gaze, allowing the suspense to build. "Dan has made contact with the Cobras."

There was a sudden silence. Stephens, puzzled at this reaction, looked uneasily around the room. He patted his pocket handkerchief, fingered his pipe and cleared his throat. Freeman sat quietly; he was not puzzled.

"Dan, this contact with the Cobras," Stephens had said just prior to the meeting, "will really sell the board members on you. Not," he added hastily, "that they aren't already. But no one expected a contact with the Cobras so soon after you joined us; this is really good news."

Freeman watched their ambivalence fill the room like a white velvet fog. White liberals to a man, with the single exception of Burkhardt, the hardheaded business member. Among them, Roger Thompson, professor of sociology at the University of Chicago, a professional white liberal who had devoted a career to proving that the inequities of Negroes were social and cultural, rather than racial; Stephens, an amateur white liberal turned pro. They can forgive a nigger almost anything other than competence, thought Freeman behind his mask. They want their choice to have been an act of charity for a Negro not quite up to the job; they want me to fumble, stumble, turn to them for help. They would like the Washington Freeman, he was a good boy. Part of them wants me to vindicate their choice of a spade for the position, but another part wants me to prove once again that it is spade incompetence, not white racism, which is responsible for the scene. They'll use me, but they'll never like me.

"That is good news, Steve," said Professor Thompson. "But are you certain this is a positive contact?"

Stephens, sensing difficulties, threw the ball to Freeman. "Dan?"

Freeman regarded a point midway across the polished mahogany conference table, frowning in thought; then he leaned forward sincerely and looked deeply into Professor Thompson's contact lenses.

"Of course, Professor, it is too early to be positive; I advocate caution at this point and I'm moving slowly. But, I made the first contact with the gang leaders several weeks ago in their poolroom headquarters; I've played pool with them almost nightly and they've visited my apartment several times since."

"Visited your apartment? Well, that is a real foot in the door. What are your immediate plans?"

"Standard procedure for a while; gain their trust and confidence, offer them an adult male to trust and admire, since they are almost all from broken homes and have none otherwise." He motioned to Stephens's colored secretary, who moved around the table gracefully, placing a folder in front of each member.

"You'll recognize that concept as your own, Professor. I've taken the liberty of including copies of the article you did concerning it for *Atlantic* a few years back, in these folders. In addition, there are biographic character sketches of the three gang leaders, Dean, Davis and Scott, plus shorter ones of several other key gang members. There is the table of organization of the gang, including the chain of command and a brief history of the Cobras as a ghetto social institution. My own plans for the gang, subject, of course, to change, are also included."

He watched them look through the folder from behind his Grecian mask, a black Prometheus among the gods, who had stolen the secret of fire from Olympus by the Potomac and was teaching its use to his people. Not the fire next time, he thought, but the fire right now. How long before they chained him, to let the black and white vultures tear at his liver?

Professor Thompson looked up. "I notice you plan a sports program for the Cobras. Hasn't that approach been pretty much discredited in reaching street-corner society?"

"In general, yes, Professor; however, I think it might tend to work with the Cobras. As you know, they emphasize sports far more than usual for a street gang. Almost every member is a pretty good athlete and they still call themselves the Cobras ASC, Athletic and Social Club. And the gang leaders were all star athletes until they dropped out of high school.

"I thought I might start with a program which would appeal to both their combativeness and athletic ability." He paused. "I'm seriously considering organizing a judo club."

"Judo?" exclaimed Burkhardt. "Isn't that just asking for trouble? Think of what they could do with that knowledge in gang fights."

"On the contrary, Mr. Burkhardt; the judoka has a strict discipline, intrinsic in the training, that he will avoid a fight whenever possible, and when offered no choice, restrain himself." Then, striking at Burkhardt's soft spot, a fanaticism concerning guns and marksmanship, he continued:

"It's almost identical to the principle employed in weapons training; by teaching gun discipline and a respect for the weapon and its potential, you tend to reduce, rather than increase, the possibility of its indiscriminate use."

"Yes, I see what you mean, Freeman. Certainly I've seen the positive effect of weapons training on antisocial types when I was in the army. It might work, at that."

"I actually got the idea from your article in *American Rifleman*," said Freeman.

"It was in the August issue," said Burkhardt, surprised, pleased and flattered. "You read it?"

"I've made it a point to read everything both you and Professor Thompson have written; it gives me an insight in your approach to the foundation's work." Burkhardt relaxed and smiled at Freeman for the first time in his memory. Got your nose open now, you little motherfucker, and it would really be beautiful if I could talk you into coaching a rifle team made up of the Cobras; but that can wait.

They discussed the Cobras for some time and then adjourned the meeting. Later, over luncheon, Stephens expressed his pleasure.

"A masterful presentation, Dan; you'd do well in advertising if you ever left the social welfare game. And, I couldn't be more pleased in your finally breaking through with Burkhardt. I think we've earned another round of martinis." He motioned to the waitress.

In the early stages of his training and organization, Freeman often used the street for his classes. He would stand casually on the street corner, "hanging out," and pass along his CIA-bred knowledge.

"You already said, Turk, it's firepower, not marksmanship in a fire fight; so how come all this jazz about range and wind and that shit?" asked Scott one afternoon.

"Because everybody has to double up as snipers. Even the cats who can't shoot will have nuisance value. Nobody likes to walk around in the dark and not know when somebody is going to shoot at him."

"Anyway, like Turk say, ain't nothing to figurin' range in a city. The length of a block, distance between lamppoles and telephone poles is all standard," said Dean.

"In an attack you'll be on battle sights, three hundred yards. It will handle anything you're likely to be shooting at; but for sniper work you try to figure the range to the inch." He paused, to make sure he had their attention.

"If you were working as a sniper from that corner building and we were the target, how would you figure the range?" He let them puzzle it a minute, then asked their resident mathematician: "Sugar?"

"I guess I'd estimate by sight from up there."

"NG; no good. Range estimation at night is always tricky, and with artificial light, too." He shook his head. "Hell, man, it's simple geometry. You know the height of the building."

"Yeah," said Scott, "yeah, and I know the distance from the base of the building to here."

"So, what's the distance of the third side of the triangle?" Smiling broadly, Scott gave the range to the inch.

"That's all right for him, Turk, but what about the rest of us?" Stud Davis asked.

"Nothing to it, Stud. Hips can run it down for you in ten minutes."

"Man, I never could do anything with math in school."

"That's because you never had educational motivation before. Take over, Sugar, and don't let 'em go until they know how to do it; then you each pass it along to the cells. Easy." He walked away.

Freeman continued to use the streets for his training, but as the weather grew cooler, he would use the poolroom after closing, or his own apartment. His close relationship with the gang leaders was completely in keeping with his cover and only added to his prestige as an active, energetic and imaginative social worker. He gradually gained their confidence and growing affection and the masks they wore for the outside world were loosened for Freeman, their personality traits becoming increasingly clear.

They had been gifted athletes and had delayed dropping out of high school only because of their love of sports. Dean, the smallest one of them, had not played football but had been that rarest of American Negro athletes, a distance runner. Few Negroes in the United States have had any taste for duplicating in a distance run the exact kind of pain and endurance they face in their daily lives. But Dean ran as he lived, methodically, impassively, the intensity he hid so well flashing only at the finish of a race, when, head back, teeth bared, he would sprint the last three or four hundred yards, punishing his black wiry body, regardless of how far he might be in front or how hopeless his pursuit of a leading opponent. But he seldom lost, except in open meets against older, more experienced men. "Ain't but one place in a race," he would say. "First place. Second and third don't count." He had a sharp, methodical mind and was temperamentally opposed to making hasty decisions. "Lemme think about it," he would say when a problem arose, and sometimes days later, when others had forgotten, he would present his opinion and it would usually be accepted without question.

One night in the poolroom after it had closed, Freeman was discussing the table of organization of the Cobra underground.

"Turk," said Dean, "that the same we always been."

"Right," said Freeman. "The only change is here, where you had a duplication." He pointed to the blackboard. "The organization was already together and there's no need to change the chain of command or the T. & O. Ordinarily, it would take three to five years to organize an underground organization of this type from scratch, but the Cobras have always been an underground."

"How do you mean?" asked Dean.

"What do you think?" countered Freeman. "We discussed the characteristics of an underground revolutionary movement last week."

"Well, secrecy. Not even all the gang members know how big the Cobras is, and the fuzz sure as hell don't. We got organization and . . . what's that word you used?"

"Motivation?"

"Yeah, motivation. And, we got discipline and we got balls."

"Right! And there are at least five or six other gangs who fit that description, not as well as the Cobras, but well enough for recruitment once our training is complete. Got any idea who they might be?"

"Let's see; the Comanches, the Apaches, the Blood Brothers on the Wes' Side," said Stud Davis.

"The Crusaders and the Tigers," said Dean.

"The Tigers!" said Davis. "Man, they don't do nothing but give parties; they even got chicks in the gang, the Tigerettes."

"You ever try to crash one of them parties?" asked Dean. "Man, them chicks as bad as they are!"

"Right," said Freeman. "And we can use women; they can often go places and do things men can't do. There are a couple of other possibilities, but those gangs top the list. How many do you figure if we recruit them all, including the Cobras?"

"More than five hundred," said Scott.

"Yeah, and what do you think five hundred well-trained revolutionaries can do to this town?"

"Turn it inside out," said Davis. They looked at one another, impressed.

"Shit, Turk," said Dean, "you don't play, do you?"

"I sure as hell don't. And not just Chicago, but every city with a ghetto, which is every major city in the north. The members of the recruitment and training cell move out in January, their cities are already selected as well as the first gangs they contact."

"You're gon' turn this country upside down," said Dean.

"Wrong. *We're* going to turn this country upside down."


"You really dig the Cobras, don't you, Daddy?" Freeman asked him one day as they stood in front of the poolroom late one lazy warm afternoon: the people were moving slowly through the streets, standing in clusters talking softly, occasionally waving to a friend, sometimes detaching themselves from one group to join another—the ghetto sounds, smells and colors, white teeth in dark faces below the sunglasses which hid them from the cold, hard world, protection for people born to the sun but forced to live in the sunless garbage heap of a sad, sunless, sick society.

"Yeah, the Cobras the best. Everybody know that. You know, one of the cats moved to New York and they know our rep way out there. Cats start gettin' bad 'cause he new on the block—you know, to find out if he got any balls. 'Where you from, nigger? Think you bad?' That kind of shit. And he told 'em he from Chicago and he a Cobra and, man, he owned the block after that. He the leader of a gang there now."

"Groovy," said Freeman, always alert to potential recruits. "If they check out, maybe we can use them for our New York scene. Harlem or Bedford-Stuyvesant?"

"Harlem."

"Go on, how'd you become a Cobra?"

"I never thought I'd be one. You know, I was really little and skinny then and I wasn't worth a shit in sports. I got better all of a sudden, but I was never as good as Stud or Hips or Pretty Willie; them cats can do anything. I was good with my hands, though." He smiled. "You know if you can't fight out here in the streets, you sure better be able to run and I never been too fast." He did not have great straightaway speed, but he did possess the quality coaches call quickness, great speed of hands and the ability to change direction instantly. It had made Dean an excellent play-making basketball guard in spite of his lack of height.

"I was only 'bout ten or eleven and the Cobras used to like to watch me fight. Sometimes they set up a fight with somebody. I had good moves even then. Seem like I always knew how to hook. You know that a tough thing for a little kid to do; the other punches easy, but a real good hook ain't easy for a little kid, but I had it. They used to talk 'bout my left hand and make bets and stuff. Next thing I know they make me the mascot and then they start using me to wiggle through windows and things when they hit a store or something and then I get to be a Cobra." He said it as if it were the most important thing that had ever happened to him.

"You ever think there might not be any Cobras one day?"

Dean looked surprised, then a bit shocked. "What you mean?"

"I mean we could all get wasted, every one of us." Freeman's gaze swept the street and he motioned to the people there. "I mean all of us. Nobody knows what whitey might do when the deal goes down."

"I never thought about that." Dean looked at the people in the street with new interest.

"Does it scare you?" asked Freeman.

"I don't know. Does it scare you?" He looked at Freeman intently.

"Hell, yeah. But that ain't nothing new. I been scared all my life. There ain't a nigger living who doesn't know fear; we live in it all our lives, like a fish in water. We just have to learn how to use it."

Dean took out a pack of cigarettes and offered Freeman one. He waved his refusal and watched two men across the street deep in an argument. A crowd was gathering, waiting for the explosion.

Freeman pointed to them: "They're scared; that's why they might kill one another in a minute. Watch 'em."

They were serious now, not loud-talking anymore, their voices low and deadly and already they had dropped that right foot back and stood aslant one another in a position for instant combat. They kept their hands ready for attack or defense, each awaiting some move from the other. Damn near the deadliest people in the world, thought Freeman, but killing each other all these years instead of the people who put all that fear and anger inside them. Finally, one said something and the other laughed and they both stood there, their heads flung back and threw their dark laughter to the sky. The crowd joined in and others threw in jokes and asides, the smiles broad in their faces, the tension suddenly gone and giving the laughter its force and power. The two men strode into a bar and the crowd moved on to other diversions.

"They got a blues about that—'laughing to keep from cryin',' it says. And that about says it. A man could get to be a philosopher listening to the blues. If we ever forget how to laugh we're finished."

"You really dig spades, don't you, Turk?"

"Yeah. I feel about spades the way you feel about the Cobras; they're my family. I got a family of twenty-five million people." He smiled. "Ain't no way I can ever be lonely."

But he was lonely, his cover, his plans had forced him into himself and his loneliness ate at him like a cancer. Always the iron control, even when drunk, the cover everything, himself nothing, afraid even when he cried out in orgasm that he might give something away.

Only with the Cobras could he be open, but he knew he used them as well. Sometimes he looked at their faces, trying to etch their features into his memory, knowing that many, if not all of them, would not survive; knowing also that they had no future otherwise: the endless waiting in the lines, unemployment lines with sullen blank, black faces at their end, the white man boss in his office, memoranda on his desk to get tougher, cut down the unemployment rolls, force them out into the streets and into the other lines leading to an employment office where there were jobs only for white faces. Junk, jail or junk and jail and more junk available for those with the price in the county jail; the guards the safest pushers in the city—"they can't bust you in the slam"—the junkies' joke between heroin nods. An aborted marriage to a favorite fuck and another black baby with no hope and no future in the land of milk and honey, replete with goodies in white plastic cases for God's own children with white plastic faces.

They moved toward the poolroom, walking slowly through the warm streets.

"That laughter, baby, is the best insurance whitey has. Once we stop laughing and singing, stop killing each other and start killing him—forget it!"

He was amazed at how quickly they learned. He pushed them ruthlessly, relentlessly, and each time they reached the saturation point, they swelled to absorb more. He had figured on eighteen months to two years, but gradually he felt sure they could begin the next summer. He did not allow himself to think of it after so many years of lonely planning; that perhaps now it was only a matter of months.

They reached the poolroom and walked inside, past the never silent television set. He glanced at the set and watched Ernie Banks wiggle his spikes solidly into the dirt of the batter's box and set his long, lithe body for the pitch.

They walked to the table in the rear and began to shoot.

"Turk, lot of the cats 1-A; what happen when they get called? They go underground?"

"No. Shit, the army is our postgraduate course, the best training ground we have; they can teach us the skills we need in a fraction of the time I can. When they get a call, have them check with you; then we go over what we need and they go and volunteer for the next call. That way they can pick their training and not get stuck in some unit that's a waste for us. Armor is a waste, unless it's armored infantry. You know what we need: skill with small arms, demolitions, small unit tactics . . ." He paused and smiled. "There's a certain poetry in whitey training us to mess with him. Every black cat in Vietnam is a potential asset for our thing. Whitey knew what he was doing when he wouldn't let us fight in the Second World War." He paused to line up a shot, stroked and missed. He watched Dean as he chalked his cue.

"You know, American white folks got more nerve than anybody; they call them gooks and us niggers, out there in Vietnam and in Korea when I was there. And they don't see any reason why the gooks and niggers shouldn't kill one another for whitey's benefit. The hang-up is that's exactly what's happening. You can't criticize success, now, can you?"

"They pretty smart, ain't they?" smiled Dean.

"Don't know whether they're smart or we're stupid. Maybe a little bit of both."

The discipline, always good, tightened and the pride increased, no longer flamboyant, but quieter, cooler. The Cobras walked tall and ready, afraid of nothing. They even lost interest in pot.

"Tell the cats to turn on every now and then; they get like suburban boy scouts and everybody will get suspicious," he told Dean. Then he smiled, remembering pot had become as popular in the suburbs as swallowing goldfish or college panty raids had once been.

They drilled endlessly in weapons training, unarmed combat, demolition theory. He taught them the theory of resistance to torture.

"Most people can't stand up under it and there's no shame if you can't; but if you give in too quick, they won't believe you and they'll keep it up. You have to hold out long enough to convince them the info you give out is for real; otherwise, the scene goes on and you haven't gained a thing.

"What you have to remember is the cats who torture enjoy it; they don't want you to quit too soon, so you have to hold on long enough for them to get their kicks, then tell them what they want to hear. Just whitey all over again. You know when he's putting you down, he don't dig it if you take low too soon."

They gradually built up a network of safe houses, arms caches and message drops. Only Freeman knew the entire network; the rest were divided between Dean, Scott and Davis. He tried to figure a way for training with handguns, then dismissed the idea as one which would attract too much attention. Besides, the kind of fighting he had in mind would find that kind of weapon almost useless.

Professor Thompson, who was writing a book on the activities of the foundation, decided to add a chapter concerning Freeman's work in contacting and defusing the Cobras. Freeman was becoming known as a bright young man in social work. He was named as an eligible bachelor in *Ebony*'s annual listing, pictured leaning suavely against his Lotus. Since he was careful to direct credit toward Stephens, remaining modest and unassuming, refusing to flirt with the white women at the integrated Hyde Park cocktail parties, arriving early and leaving early, before the potent cocktails might provoke an unpleasant scene, always appearing with women dark enough not to be mistaken for white, he was pointed out as an example of a Negro who was making it in American society.

No one could imagine that Freeman, tame, smug and self-satisfied, would ever rock the boat, much less suspect that he planned to sink it.

# 10

The first time Freeman hinted what he planned for them, Stud picked it up immediately. "Man, you know the first time shit like that start happenin' they going come lookin' for the Cobras."

"No they won't," replied Freeman.

"No? How come? We about the only gang over here with that kinda balls, and the fuzz know it."

"They won't come looking for you because junkies don't do what we're going to do and starting very soon, the King Cobras is going to be the most turned-on gang in Chicago."

The street-gang wars in New York in the late fifties, which threatened the entirety of the city and which were increasingly difficult for the police to control, ended primarily for one reason: junk. Junkies don't fight, except in desperation for a fix.

The word spread among the police that the King Cobras were toying with "horse"; with some relief the police waited for the addiction to take hold. It would mean an increase in petty theft, but as long as it did not spill outside of the ghetto and it was nigger stealing from nigger, it meant no extra work.

The symptoms were there: upon being searched, there was an increasing amount of gang members with hypo scars on the forearm, the pupils dilated by drugs. Police were informed when receiving their cut from dope pushers that the Cobras were becoming excellent customers. The scars were from unsterilized hypodermic needles, the dilated pupils from pot. The heroin was refined and resold in New York at a slight loss, or a profit, depending on whether the narcotics men had busted an incoming shipment from abroad. The Cobras overnight became a nonbopping gang; still dangerous when their turf was invaded, but no longer aggressive. Police duty in their area became almost tame, consisting of the collection

of graft, confinement of crime and violence to the area and the head whippings which are routine for any cop working in the ghetto.

Freeman's contact with the gang had been duly noticed and he was
personally commended for his positive influence at a meeting of the board
of directors of the foundation. The pacifying influence of heroin was not
mentioned. Freeman did not assign a street worker to the Cobras, but
worked with them himself. He often wondered at the reaction of the Board
had they known what his program of rehabilitation actually entailed.

The gang organization was perfect for his purpose. The Cobras had
already been an underground organization, visible only in their moments
of violence, closed off to the outside world otherwise. Freeman built on
the original organizational structure, following the same chain of command, utilizing the already rigid discipline and introducing refinements
borrowed from the French Maquis, the Israeli, Cypriot and Yugoslav
underground movements. The training proceeded more rapidly than he
had anticipated, since for the first time in most of their lives the members
of the King Cobras had educational motivation.

Stud remained Freeman's and the Cobras' field commander and Dean
revealed why he had become the gang leader. He had a tendency to shuck
the world, to pretend mental stagnation while in actuality he possessed
a methodical, analytical mind, much more cautious and steady than that
of the mercurial Davis. Freeman had to fight against hero worship since
he was the only outsider who had ever demonstrated a genuine interest
in them as human beings.

"Look, goddamnit, there ain't no head niggers in this outfit! The whole
scene is designed to have the man below move up at least three steps
whenever necessary. If I go, Do-Daddy takes over and right on down the
line. Every nigger revolt in the history of America has ended when they
wasted the head nigger. That won't happen with us.

"I am the Man and you do what I say, but when they get to me, don't
look back, dig? No tears, no flowers, just keep fucking with whitey."

He spent a great deal of time with his three lieutenants in his apartment, and when they relaxed in the new surroundings they asked exhaustive
questions about each of his paintings, carvings and sculptures. One day he
pointed out quietly that the majority of his collection had been created by

men who were not white. They devoured whatever he told them about the history of their people in America. Somehow, they had attained a pride in themselves as human beings based on their contempt and hatred of the white man and a stubborn pride in their toughness and defiance. Now he told them that theirs was a history and tradition of which they could be proud.

"Man, we took everything they laid on us—slavery, lynchings, segregation, the worst damn jobs, the worst damn food—and come up swinging. We been on our ass, but never on our knees and that's what the white man don't understand. He thinks it's the same thing."

He told them about their history, where in Africa their ancestors had lived, the cultural heritage the white man had destroyed, forbidding them their language, their music, their sculpture, carving and painting, their dancing and giving them nothing in return.

"No, not even their jive white man's religion. Less than one-sixth of the freed men upon emancipation had been allowed to become Christians and they justified slavery on the basis of converting the heathen."

He told them of their heroes and heroines, of the countless slave revolts, Nat Turner, Denmark Vesey, Sojourner Truth, countless other names they had not been taught in the propaganda that passes for American history. He remembered his own introduction to the history of the Negro in America by a proud black teacher of music, who in defiance of the rules devoted time to teach them some pride in themselves and their people; who taught them to distrust the image the white man thrust at them in the movies, on the radio and in their history texts. He remembered how he had to descend to the bowels of the library in East Lansing, passing the books written by the "name" American historians in his search for the truth about his people. Now he passed it along. Each cell meeting devoted part of its time to the history of the American Negro.

"We got no time for hate; it's a luxury we can't afford. Whitey just stands in the way of freedom and he has to be moved any damn way we can; he doesn't mean any more than that."

All the time he spoke to them of their mission he was aware of the inconsistencies in his arguments, the humor and horror in what they intended, the hell they would create for their people in the struggle for their freedom. He wondered how long this would last, how long before he

began believing each word as if the word of God? Would it be when he
finally had the power of life and death, when the resources of the city and
perhaps the nation were devoted to finding and destroying him? How long
before he saw himself as a black Messiah?

Freeman knew from the personnel records at CIA that an agent became
burned-out when he no longer had an identity as a distinct personality;
after the erosion of the years of cover, constantly becoming someone different, finally wore away what he actually was, until he no longer knew
what he was. Freeman had been playing roles for whites and finally for
everyone. How long before the edges of his cover and those of his personality would blur, merge, and he could no longer tell where one began
and the other ended?

That was why it was an advantage to be black. There were millions of
peoples and races in Europe whose centuries of subservience made them
culturally perfect as raw material for spying. The nigger was the only natural agent in the United States, the only person whose life might depend,
from childhood, on becoming what whites demanded, yet somehow
remaining what he was as an individual human being. Freeman had had
years of practice at the game before adopting the cover he had assumed
at the CIA and the present cover as a playboy of the midwestern world.
That might save him, but it was important nevertheless that he establish
an organization which would survive him. Once they discovered him, he
would disappear. There would be no martyr-making trials and no more
public assassinations as with Malcolm X. He would just disappear and
the white man, confident in the eternal passivity and stupidity of the
Negro, except for rare individual exceptions, would assume that the organization would die with Freeman. It must not be so.

He read them their poets and their literature. He played their music.
They knew the doo-waps, rock and roll, rhythm and blues, but jazz was
something played for white folks in clubs in the Loop or in concert halls. He
wondered how some of the jazz musicians would feel if they knew how far
away many of their people felt they were. He remembered the days when
Negroes in Chicago were allowed to work, before the stockyards moved
west to the right-to-work-law states and before the steel mills and other
plants automated, before the railroads cut back and laid off. There was jazz

on the South Side, played by Negroes for Negroes. Of all those clubs, only the Drexel Hotel lounge survived. He used expense-account money to take them there to hear Miles Davis. Miles had always played the South Side, in the Pershing Ballroom and the smoky bars on Sixty-third before they went rock and roll, when he was blowing so much stuff the whites couldn't understand it until one day, after years of neglect, they rediscovered him and he asked what was all the noise, he always played like that.

They listened to Miles's records and to Lady Day, Pres, Monk, Diz and the rest, and began hearing things in jazz that they had heard in rhythm and blues. They listened to down-home blues. He became the father and big brother they had never had and, although he fought it, he returned their affection and love. He knew this could be a fatal weakness, but he could not help it. He watched them grow now that they had a purpose, and found it sad that there was nothing for them in this land where their ancestors had lived for hundreds of years, except destruction; but in that negative urge to strike out against oppression they had found something that freed them from their fears and the doubts about themselves and their color. He watched them grow and become more human and knew that their newfound humanity would not inhibit their becoming the killers he was training them to be.

He taught them all the tricks of the trade and knew that if he had organized a network as quickly, silently and efficiently in the field, he would have been commended. They had not been tested, but he had no doubt about their performance once they were. Already they were impatient to begin. He told them they would begin operating during the coming summer under cover of the inevitable rioting. He knew as surely as the sun rises that the cops who occupied the ghetto would not give up their pastime of whipping niggers' heads in spite of directions from above concerning less physical means of arrest and investigation in the ghetto. They were not convinced, those thickheaded cops, that niggers would tolerate no more head whippings. The cops felt sure that the answer to the riots and the increasing lack of respect for the uniform was more blood, more stitches, more battered kidneys. Leopards do not change their spots and ghetto cops do not stop whipping heads. There would be riots during the coming summer and his network would be there experiencing their baptism of fire.

"The whole world will be watching us and if we can survive even a year they'll look like fools. And nothing bugs the American white man more than looking like a fool."

"Well, you know I don't mind making whitey look like a fool," Dean said. "And you know I'm with you all the way. But do you really think we got a chance of winning?"

"Who said anything about winning? We don't have to win; what we have to do is get down to the nitty-gritty and force whitey to choose between the two things he seems to dig more than anything else: fucking with us and playing Big Daddy to the world."

"Makes sense, Turk. But how we going to force him to choose?" asked Scott.

"By tying up so many of his troops here in the States and stretching him so thin economically that he discovers he can't do both at the same time. And don't ever think he's not so hooked on messing with us that he won't do anything to keep the scene the way it's always been: us on our ass and him digging it. He could go all the way: barbed wire, concentration camps, gas ovens; a 'final solution' of the Negro problem." He paused to listen to the stereo; Billie Holiday was singing "God Bless the Child."

"'Pappa may have and Mamma may have, but God bless the child that's got his own.' Dig that? We got to get our own! But before we can, we got to get that black nigger pride working for us. We put it away like sharecroppers put away their best most precious things.

"You know how the people are who come up from the South. Down inside that big trunk with the big lock, wrapped up inside tissue paper and cotton batting, and maybe nowadays in foam rubber and saran wrap, they got at least one thing they brought along from down South, one thing they couldn't leave behind, that they cherish above all else. It's too precious to even take out every now and then to look at and feel, but they know it's there.

"Well, that nigger pride is like that. We wrapped it up and put it away inside that trunk, inside a cedar chest, wrapped up in paper and cotton, mothballs, with a big lock on the outside, waiting for a day when we'd need it. We got to get inside that trunk and get it out or find out if it's empty. White folks been trying to rob that trunk for centuries and maybe they did and we didn't know it, or it shriveled up and disappeared out of disuse. But if we can find it and use it, if we can get that black pride going for us, then nothing is going to stop us until we're free—nothing and nobody. They'll have to kill us or free us, twenty-five million of us!

"It's gone on long enough. Now's the time to say: no more, baby; it stops right here. They got very short memories about what they been doing to us since slavery and if you don't believe we've had it made from the first time they brought us over, crammed into those boats, ask whitey.

"Remember all those plantation movies? You can see them every night on television nowadays."

Stud Davis straightened, tilted an imaginary planter's hat to the correct angle on his head, puffed on a long imaginary cheroot.

"Boy, I say theah, boy!" Davis said, waving expansively toward the seated Cobras, speaking in a parody of the southern cultured drawl of the Hollywood bourbon aristocrat. Scott, the comedian of the three, took his cue and, leaping to his feet, approached Stud in a sidewise shuffle.

"Now, who dat, say who dat, when I say who dat? Why, lawdy, if it ain't Mr. Beauregard, come home from de wah."

"Bless me, it's George, my faithful old slave retainer. But, George," said Beauregard-Davis, choking with emotion, "you're free now. You're not a slave, anymore."

"Free? Dat bad, massa? I gwine need a doctor?"

"No, George, it means you're not my slave anymore; you can leave the plantation, go anywhere you wish."

"But I don't want to leave, Mr. Beauregard."

"But I can't pay you, George; the carpetbaggers have ruined me."

"Well, now, don't worry none 'bout paying me. Why, I wouldn't rightly know what to do with money. I jes' want to stay right here with you, Mr. Beauregard, hee, hee." He turned and shuffled off. The others were weak with laughter.

"You don't think it wasn't like that, read your history books. But somewhere we scared them. Think about it: everyone they tried to work those fields in the hot sun dropped like flies and then they started bringing us over from Africa. It didn't matter how many of us died as long as we lasted through a crop, because they figured on an endless supply.

"We down on that big plantation when they first start bringing the slaves over, the one in all the movies with the happy niggers who never want to be free. They bring in those niggers from Charleston or Savannah— first nigger slaves to be worked in that area. Cat owns the plantation is progressive, see, so he's conducting this southern scientific agricultural experiment."

They were all standing now, as if on the street corner talking trash, the commedia dell'arte of the ghetto.

"Yeah, man," said Stud, "MGM in technicolor. Big-ass house, look like the White House, big porch on the front, big white pillars."

"Yeah," said Scott. "Barefoot darky sittin' on the steps plunkin' a banjo."

"And singin' a spiritual," said Dean. "Never no blues in the movies; white folks scared of that, but a spiritual talkin' 'bout how good it going to be when they dead. They got a big magnolia tree in the yard."

"And big-ass double doors 'bout twenty feet high; and inside, in the hall, a big chandelier and a winding staircase."

"Naw, man, a big curved double staircase."

"And downstairs," said Freeman, "Massa Charlie waiting for his wife, dressed in white."

"Smoking a cigar this long and this skinny. Black string tie and a long coat with a center vent up to here."

"Yeah, cat with the side vents and long sideburns is the bad guy. And maybe he got on a fancy vest, yellow silk."

"Then the chick standin' up there on top of the stairs."

"She a blonde or maybe a redhead; the chick with black hair is the bitch who digs the cat and gets somebody to waste him, but she changes her mind and jumps in front of the good guy and gets burned instead."

"Yeah, the good chick ain't never got black hair. She got one of them little umbrellas with the ruffles."

"They call 'em parasols."

"Yeah, little-ass parasol and a floppy hat with a big ribbon down to her ass."

"Wide skirt and she all pink, maybe. Pink dress, pink parasol, pink cheeks; pretty little pinktoe chick."

"She come down the staircase like she floatin'."

"And the head nigger hand the cat his big brim hat."

"Yeah, nigger think he into something, don't never smile. But his handkerchief-head old lady always sassin' the white folks and the head nigger don't dig it."

"Groovy," said Freeman, "you got the picture. They go out into the yard and the carriage is there. Two horses."

"Not black; that's for the bad cat. Brown. The carriage real shiny with red or yellow spokes on the wheels. Nigger with a straw hat in his hand holdin' the horses."

"They going out into the cotton fields to see how many niggers died since the sun come up; you know, property inventory. They get out into them technicolor fields and the niggers ain't dead, they singing, baby. Singing and laughing and them white folks don't know if they laughing at them," said Freeman.

"You think them white folks weren't scared? You think that didn't flip them out? Out there in them fields where everybody else been dropping like flies, niggers singing and swinging. You think they didn't want to stop that song; that they still don't have to stop that song? Well, baby, we're gonna sing and nobody's going to shut us up; we're going to sing a freedom song, loud enough for the whole world to hear. We're going to open up that trunk and get out that black pride." He was silent, lost in his thoughts. They watched him cross the room and mix a drink.

"You cats don't listen to spirituals anymore; they taught you to be ashamed, but the message is there: 'Go down Moses and set my people free . . .' What people you think they were talking about?

"Man, it's all there if you listen. You can't find your history in the white man's books. If you want to know your history, listen to your music. Remember that spade poetry I read you last week?" He recited:

*"Why do we wait so long on the marble steps, blood falling from*
    *our open wounds?*
*And why do our black faces search the empty sky?*
*Is there something we have forgotten?*
*Something we have lost wandering in strange lands?"*

Freeman paused and looked at them. "Yeah, we lost something; we lost our freedom. And we forgot something, too. We forgot how to fight." He looked at each of them in turn. "Waste the Comanches!"

"The Comanches? What do you mean, Turk?" asked Dean.

"I've been holding you back too long. It's time to find out what you can do. You've been complaining about the Comanches saying you don't have balls anymore, invading your turf, messing with your chicks, calling you junkies and punks. You don't do something the fuzz got to get suspicious; no way you could get that tame so fast.

"Stud, you set it up, you ain't supposed to be on nothing except some heavy pot, anyway, so it will figure to be your scene. Put out the word you want to rumble. Daddy will supervise, Stud's field commander. Insist on no heats; just fists if you can get it, but that's not so important. Try not to kill anybody if you can help it, and don't forget what I taught you.

"OK, split. I got to get ready for a date."

They filed out of his apartment, excited and already discussing plans for the fight.

The Cobras and the Comanches met in a vacant lot flanking the elevated railroad tracks of the Santa Fe railroad. The fight lasted less than twenty minutes. There were less than ten Comanches still standing, willing and able to fight, by the time Stud recalled his fighters with a single shrill whistle of command. Stud reported to Freeman the following day.

"Was as easy as eatin' soul food, Turk. We wasted the cats so quick they still trying to figure out what happened. But I didn't get no kicks just runnin' things; Daddy better for that kind of scene."

"You just bugged, Stud, because you couldn't get with it. You'll have plenty of fighting pretty soon. Right now, cool it. Anybody hurt?"

"Naw. We cooled it, like you said. Pretty Willie didn't let a cat loose soon enough and think he broke his arm. Heard it crack. Man, that judo shit you teach us as good as a blade."

"Pretty Willie, huh?"

"Yeah. You know how he get when he in a fight. He the baddest cat in the Cobras, 'cept for me. When he really mean, you got to kill him to stop him. You know, I think the reason he so evil because he so light; I really think that cat want to be black as you can get. Always got the blackest chick he can find, won't look at a light-skin chick. Before he joined the gang and we started riding him 'bout being so light, you couldn't even talk about his color without a fight. He better now, but he still hung up."

"OK, Stud, cool it. Tell the cats I said they did a good job." Freeman turned and walked down the street, thinking about Pretty Willie du Bois.

Pretty Willie was a problem Freeman had to solve, because he was potentially one of the leaders of the underground, one who might be trusted to command an underground unit in another city himself. The gang had helped in bringing it "right down front." Teasing him about the color of his skin, joking that he thought himself better than the rest because he was so pretty.

If Freeman could find some way to get him over that psychological hurdle, Willie would be a field officer as valuable as Stud Davis. He had to find the key. Pretty Willie had improved, as had all of the members of the gang recruited into Freeman's underground, but there was still too much of the brooding about his lack of pigment to trust him to lead others. Freeman saw him as a potential leader of his top cell, his elite guard commander, second in command to Stud Davis.

Sugar Hips was an undeveloped natural mathematician, a genius with figures. In any except a ghetto school his genius would have been recognized and nurtured. In the overcrowded classrooms, where the sheer job of maintaining discipline precluded any except the most dedicated of teachers teaching, Sugar Hips Scott was a nuisance. He was far too far ahead of the other students, did his problems too quickly and was bored with the level of mathematics with which he was forced to deal. He had dropped out of school at sixteen, in disgust. He went through the geometry, algebra and calculus texts that Freeman got for him from the University of Chicago library with a speed and alacrity that amused Freeman and awed others of the Cobras.

There was not a day when Freeman did not curse the talent and intelligence within the Cobras that had been stifled. And for the simple reason, he thought time and again, that they are black.

Scott was his logistics officer, Davis his battle commander, Dean his second-in-command. Pretty Willie du Bois could be his best fighting commander, if he could just find the key to free him from his hang-up about his color. Within a week of the rumble, Freeman thought that he had discovered that key.

# 11

"**W**e need a propagandist," said Freeman. "I hear Pretty Willie can write."

They nodded in agreement. "You want to see him now, Turk?" asked Dean.

"Yeah, where can I find him?"

"Prob'ly in his pad in Hyde Park."

"I know where it is. I'll see you later."

He drove to Willie's pad; it was a basement apartment located in a half-court building. He walked down the short flight of steps and knocked on the door.

"Who it is?"

"Turk."

Willie opened the door. He was barefoot and wearing only a pair of tight gabardine slacks. "Come on in, Turk."

Freeman walked into the apartment. There was a long, narrow living room, a small bedroom with kitchen and bath in the rear. A tall redhead with close-cropped hair sat cross-legged on a blanket-covered mattress on the floor, smoking a reefer. She had no clothes on.

"Go home, bitch," Willie said. Without a word, she arose and walked toward the bedroom. "Wait a minute." She paused. "Turk, you want some of this?"

Freeman, looking at the Japanese prints hung on the wall, ignored him. The redhead regarded Freeman woodenly. Willie dismissed her with a wave of his hand. She came from the bedroom shortly after dressing and left.

"A fucking freak," Willie said contemptuously.

"So what are you doing with her?"

"I like to fuck with her white mind."

"Looks like you're more shook up than she is." Freeman pointed to the prints. "Nice reproductions."

"Hokusai, Hiroshige, Utamaro." Willie pointed to the prints in turn, watching Freeman closely. Freeman walked to a canvas sling chair in the corner and sat.

"Daddy tells me you write." Willie's face closed. "I'd like to see some of your stuff. It's for the scene."

Willie nodded and disappeared into the bedroom. He returned with a large attaché case, unlocked it and sat it at Freeman's feet. He went back into the bedroom while Freeman opened the case, and returned wearing a lightweight V-necked pullover. Freeman rummaged through the case. There were the portions of three novels and more than a dozen short stories of varying length.

"Any poetry? That'll tell me quicker what I want to know."

Willie reached into the case, pulled out a manila folder and handed it to Freeman. He reclined on the mattress on the floor and watched Freeman silently.

"We need a propagandist," explained Freeman as he opened the folder. Willie regarded him with more interest. Freeman leafed through several of the poems. He looked up at Willie. "You always write in a blues rhythm?"

"Right now, yeah. I've been trying to capture the way South Side spades talk, but for a long time it didn't work. Then I figured out they talk the way they sing, so I've been doing a lot of blues things. Most of that stuff I wrote singing." Willie pointed to a guitar case leaning in the corner.

"When I get an idea, I switch on the tape recorder and mess around with it until it sounds right; then I play it back, write it down and rework it on paper. My dialogue is much better than before I started doing that. I can hear those blues rhythms now when I'm hanging out on the block. Funny I never thought of it that way before—spades singing when they talk."

"Whitey says we're nonverbal. Nowadays, they're teaching us English as a foreign language."

"That's his hang-up. You want some coffee?" Willie rose.

"Long as it's not instant."

"I don't drink that shit. Come on in the kitchen." Freeman followed him into the kitchen and sat reading the poetry at the kitchen table while Willie busied himself brewing the coffee. He read one poem written as if a Negro on relief were speaking to a white social worker, "Anti-Poverty Blues." He read aloud:

*"I sit here in my soul-hole,*
*forgotten,*
*like a can of black caviar on my ghetto grocer's shelf."*

Freeman nodded, read some of the other poems, glanced through some short stories.

"OK, baby," he said, "you're the propagandist. Keep the stuff like this, ironic, understated, blues things written for black folks; no shit about white devils, don't give whitey any stature by screaming what a big drag he is. Put him down and you build him up; the put-on is what we want. Keep the themes simple, few in number and then work out varieties on those; like in the blues.

"Use blues rhythms, your poetry, doggerel, anything catchy that people will remember and pass along; we want to plug into the ghetto grapevine. You understand the kind of thing we need?" Willie returned to the kitchen table with two mugs of steaming black coffee.

"Yeah," he said, "yeah, beautiful; I have some ideas already. I can let you see something next week. OK?"

"Groovy. Top security, though." Willie nodded, smiling to himself, thinking things over. "Who else would be good at this kind of thing?" Freeman asked.

"Ted, Tan-Dan and Charlie."

"Set up your own cell, you're in charge. Let Hips know what kind of equipment you need—mimeo machines, typewriters, paper, ink, office supplies. Keep your operation simple and lightweight, stuff we can move quickly and easily. Use the two-car garage on Indiana Avenue as your headquarters and scout around for alternative sites in case you have to run. Work out a budget and get the money from Hips: get as much of the stuff hot as you can and buy the rest through a dummy so it can't be traced back to you by the fuzz. You know the routine.

"We'll need leaflets, handbills, homemade bumper stickers and scripts for propaganda broadcasts. We'll use cheap transistor tape recorders for that. I want you to work out a complete propaganda program with major themes, priority target groups and including counterpropaganda for what you anticipate whitey will say about us once we begin operating."

"First thing he'll do is cry Red."

"Right. But don't spend too much time denying we're Communists. Our people will know better and we really don't care what whites will think. Also, I want you to work out an international propaganda program for distribution to overseas publications in Europe, Africa and Asia; they're not likely to get our side from the 'free' white press."

"How about artwork? Cartoons, stuff like that?"

"Excellent. Who do we have?"

"Lots of the cats can draw; no trouble there. Songs, too?"

"You have the idea. Anything to get our message across, but remember that a lot of this stuff will be done after we've gone underground and are being hunted. The more you can do now, the easier later."

"I can work up a rough outline of the whole program in about two weeks. OK?"

"Take as much time as you need and get in touch whenever you have questions."

Willie reached over and turned on the transistor radio which stood on the kitchen table; it was tuned to the station beaming its broadcasts to the ghetto. They sat silent awhile, listening to Dionne Warwick singing "Walk On By."

"Do most of the Cobras know about your Hyde Park scene, Willie?"

"Sure, they seem to dig I'm living right in the middle of whitey; particularly since what we've been planning. Daddy and Stud come by all the time; sometimes together, sometimes alone. We lollygag, maybe turn on, or cook up some soul food; we had some red beans and rice last week was out of sight." He gestured with his hand.

"This is my cover. My mother wanted me to go to one of those Louisiana excuses for schools where the pecking order is based on the lack of pigment in your skin and the lack of kink in your hair. I cooled her out by enrolling at the University and she brags about her son being a genius."

"How much time have you spent in college, Willie?"

"I seldom take a full load of credits; it gets in the way of hanging out with the boys. I guess if I added them up it would come to a little over two years."

"You intend to get a degree?"

"What for? What kind of job could I get with it? I hope you're not going to suggest I pass." His face closed again.

"I don't know what people mean by 'passing.' Being black or white in this country is a state of mind. You're black because you think black, feel black and act black. I know people who look like charcoal who are more white than whitey. But that's not the point; whoever told you a university is a vocational school, preparation for a job or career?"

"What else is it?"

"That's what it is for most of the people in this country, but in other places people feel education has an intrinsic value all its own. In most other countries an educated man is respected whether he has a crying quarter. Do you know that in Arab countries people carry a folded newspaper and a pen showing in their pockets as symbols they can read and write? And some Africans will put on their business cards the fact they flunked out of Oxford or Cambridge? The important thing is that they were there; it's not nearly so important that they didn't stay. Black people are going to have to get like that because whites are never going to share the wealth with us."

"So what's the use of getting an education if you still have to stand in that unemployment line?"

"Because you're a better man for having an education. If we ever break the vicious circle they thrust us into and really get some quality educational institutions in the ghetto, you know what they'll produce?"

"What?"

"The best educated poor people in this country; but it'll be worth it. My grandmother used to say to me: 'Get that education, boy, it's the one thing the white man can't take away from you.' And she was right. She never asked me what I was going to be, she was just delighted I kept my head in those books. Those books were symbols of freedom to her and she was right about that, too."

Willie was thoughtfully silent for a few minutes, moving his crossed foot in time to the music.

"So why all the effort if things can't improve?"

"Oh, things can improve, but there will always be two countries here: one white, rich, fat and smug; the other black, poor, lean and striving. It's not such a bad state to be in; there's a whole world out there not getting schizo because they don't keep up with the Joneses. Things can be better without being white."

"I can't figure you, Turk."

"What's to figure?"

"What are you, a Muslim, nationalist, black-power advocate, or what?"

"Willie," said Freeman and shook his head sadly, "why do you have to label me? Whitey will do it soon enough when the deal goes down. They'll come up with a lot of labels until they find the one which best puts down Uncle Tom and then all the rest will echo it. Why can't I just be a man who wants to be free, who wants to walk tall and proud on his own turf as a black man? Why can't it be as simple as that?"

"Maybe it's power. If the scene ever gets off the ground, you'll have a lot."

"Who needs it? You can't eat it, wear it or screw it. It won't even cure a hangover. How come you're in it, Willie?"

"I want to mess with whitey."

"It won't be enough; it's negative, you'll need a more positive reason than that to get you through. You ever kill a man, Willie?"

"No, but I've hurt some pretty bad in fights."

"It's not the same. When the time comes that you lay a man out with his guts spilled out in the gutter, you'll be surprised how fast hate disappears. He'll be another human being and you'll have put an end to it. You'll need some love, or something, to keep you doing that. Unless you find out you enjoy it, and I don't think you will. You better think about that. Some of the cats will enjoy it. Stud will."

"What do you mean?"

"He's a killer. He doesn't know it yet, but he is. I saw a lot in Korea. Once they get a taste of blood, nothing else gives them as much, booze, women, nothing. I don't really believe there's any justification for killing, but freedom comes as close as any."

Suddenly Willie realized something. He leaned across the table toward Freeman and placed a hand on his arm.

"You don't like any of this, do you?"

Freeman looked into his coffee cup as if searching for his soul.

"No," he replied. He rose, walked to the sink and rinsed out his cup. "I have to split."

They walked to the door.

"Come by again, Turk; I dug talking to you."

"Sure, baby." He roughed Willie's curly hair. "And don't worry about not having enough pigment. As far as I'm concerned, you're one of the blackest cats we have."

He walked out into the cool evening. He felt he'd got through to Willie, that he'd planted a seed. Willie was involved with the movement now that he had a propaganda program to create, but Freeman would have to bring the color thing down front, get it out into the open once and for all and either win him or lose him forever. He thought he knew how he could do it.

He felt restless and decided to walk most of his rounds that night. He had settled into a routine on the job, cruising or walking the streets first to judge the mood and atmosphere. Then he would stop in a favorite tavern for a beer before making his checks with his street workers. He walked Sixty-third Street that night after leaving Willie's apartment and stopped at the Boulevard Lounge.

"Hey, Dan, how you doing, baby? Friend of yours in the back," said the bartender.

"Hey, man. Friend? Who?"

"Pete Dawson. Just got back from California."

"Groovy! I've been looking for the cat since I got back to Chicago." He walked the length of the bar and entered a smaller room in the back, more intimate, with less modern and more comfortable furnishings. A small bar was tucked in one corner and Dawson sat there chatting with the bartender and three customers.

"Pete, baby! How you doing, man?"

"Freebee, good to see you! I heard you were back in town." They shook hands and punched each other's shoulders, smiling broadly. "Sit down and have a taste. You still drink scotch, don't you?" Dawson ordered drinks.

"Pete Dawson, the Sherlock of the South Side. How's the detective business?"

"Beats the post office or driving a bus."

"What were you doing so long in California?"

"I was on detached duty, attending a seminar on riot control. I'm in charge of the plainclothes section of the riot-control task force."

"Beautiful, man, you're really coming along. Get a promotion along with it?"

"Does it snow in July in Chicago?" Dawson smiled to soften the bitterness in his voice. "No, I'm still a sergeant. I read a paper at the seminar, though, and everyone seemed to dig it. The FBI requested a copy."

"What on?"

"The Chicago approach to riot control. We think we've combined the best of several plans."

"Sounds interesting. Could I take a look at it?"

"Sure. Main point is we try to get plainclothes spade cops into the area once it's been sealed off, to try and cool the crowd. We use force only when we have no other choice and then we don't play around."

Freeman thought the paper could be useful and while thinking it, hesitated. What kind of cat have I become? I'm going to use a friend and I don't even blink an eye.

"Pete, why don't you give us a rundown at the board meeting next month? I'm sure the directors will be interested. It'll be good for at least fifty bills. I'll try to get you a hundred. No sweat with your superior?"

"No; he's about as straight as they can get. Gets more bugged than me that I can't get a promotion. Let me know when you want me to come by."

"Crazy. You seen any of my street workers?"

"Yeah. Tell me they been working for a change since you took over. I saw Perkins on Sixty-third Street a few minutes ago. He usually stops in here for a brew about this time."

"They had it made before I got here. One cat was in night school and two others were working the night shift at the post office downtown. But that scene is over now. Perkins is a good one, though."

"How does it feel to be back in Chicago? Place look different?"

"No, looks the same as when we were kids and you were an Apache and I was a Cobra. Good to be home."

"Yeah, Chicago gets into your blood."

"Yeah, like leukemia." Dawson laughed and switched the pistol on his belt to a more comfortable position.

"The Cobras and the Apaches. Man, we had us some rumbles, didn't we? I still got the scar from that time I got shot." They smiled together, remembering.

"Ever see any of the cats?"

"Every now and then. Lot of 'em in the slam in Joliet. I had to bust some." Dawson looked soberly into his glass, drained it and motioned for another. "Man, that's not an easy thing to do, bust a friend."

Freeman tried to change the subject.

"Think there'll be a riot this summer?"

"Ain't there always? We've kept them small so far, but you can never tell."

"When do you think they might break loose, and where?"

"Who can tell? A good time would be when I'm on vacation catching fish in Michigan."

"You know they wouldn't do it while you're gone. They're going to give you a chance to be a hero."

"You know the only spade heroes on this police force are dead."

"That's what I mean, baby. I'll be there when they make the posthumous citation."

"Thanks, old buddy, you so good to me."

"And I'll take care of your old lady, too, after you've gone."

"Which one?"

"The one looks like twenty miles of bad road; the only one you got."

"You know the chicks always did prefer me to you."

"Prefer you going the other way." They smiled at one another.

"Freebee, good to have you back. Man, we can really swing together again."

"Like, really, baby. I better get to work. Cool it, man."

He left the bar thinking of how much fun he could have now that Dawson was back in Chicago. He also wondered how to recruit him.

# 12

It had been a harsh winter, with subzero temperatures a regular thing. There would be an occasional respite while the big, soft snow covered the city and for a short time covered the grime and dirt and ugliness of Chicago with its virginal whiteness, but within hours after the last flake fell, the virginal snow would be a greasy, dirt-grimed whorelike snow and then the temperature would drop and film the streets with mirrorlike glaze, turning the city snow into something that crunched underfoot like an old cereal in a new box labeled super and all-new. There was nothing super and all-new about Chicago and it is not a place for people who concern themselves with the weather, winter or summer. The wind would whip in from the lake, bearing airborne razors of ice that sliced the flesh. There were regular gray skies and little sun. The sky seemed to sit just above the Tribune Tower and it would sometimes descend to the city streets when the warm-air masses moved up across the plains from the Gulf of Mexico to turn the city into a fog-bound, slushy swamp full of mud-splattered people who groped their way in the dense muck, mire and moody low-sitting cloud, like amoebas in search of a guide to nowhere.

When there was sun, it would come from afar in a hazy, cloudless sky, giving a harsh, cold and biting light, the lack of clouds permitting what little warmth remained to flee toward the planets above, the people below creating little clouds of their own as they breathed and gasped, moving through the brutal city. Because the weather was so menacing, the Cobras were not missed from their usual haunts and there was no need to interrupt training by having some of the gang members on the block. It was too cold to be there and the police and social workers did not worry where they might be since the word was that the Cobras were no longer a bopping gang. And since lower-class Negroes are visible only when convenient or menacing, the Cobras disappeared and no one concerned themselves with what they might be doing that cold and forbidding winter.

They were learning the lessons of the oppressed throughout history in striking back at their oppressors; the linguistics of deception; subterfuge, to strike when least expected and then fade into the background; to hound, harass, worry and weaken the strong and whittle away at the strength and power that kept them where they were. Just before the rumble near the railroad tracks, the winter ended as abruptly as it had begun and spring was in Chicago with no warning, the flowers blooming, the trees suddenly budding, the grass turning green, the dirty snow melting and disappearing into the sewers. Spring meant baseball and track, walks in the parks for young lovers and examinations for the students reluctant to remain in the libraries and overheated apartments with textbooks that had become symbolic of the prison of a nasty Chicago winter.

It was time for examinations for Freeman's small band of revolutionaries-in-training. They were becoming restless with the constant drills, the routines; they wanted to "get it on." The rumble had convinced Freeman that they had not softened and that they could be counted on to follow orders. There were two more tests that were necessary and the change in weather permitted them.

Freeman continued to contribute to his playboy image; pretending to enjoy parties that bored him, dating women he did not like, flattering men he detested, doing and saying and acting things that sickened him. But there was never a hint that he was anything other than he appeared to be and those of his committed friends who were now active in the "movement" and who remembered Freeman as a tireless firebrand in the struggle for civil rights now regarded him with contempt as a hopeless sellout. They stopped asking him to attend meetings, contribute to their campaigns, man their picket lines or join their marches. They were his barometer and he judged his performance by their personal reaction to him. The women thought him an eligible bachelor, if a bit of a chaser. The men thought him harmless and appreciated that he did not try to steal their women; Freeman thought that there was little to choose from among the black middle-class chicks available and that risking the wrath of an insecure middle-class Negro, whose only available test of manhood was confined to the boundaries of his bed, was a waste of time and energy. Like Willy Loman, but for different reasons, it was important that Freeman be well liked, and he was.

He made speeches in the white suburbs concerning juvenile delinquency in the ghetto, as the executive director of his foundation. He knew that his speeches were intended for entertainment rather than enlightenment and he spiced them with the white man's statistics concerning Negro crime. He did not point out that Negro crime was largely confined to the ghetto, because he knew those nice white people wanted to feel threatened by the nasty Negroes in the ghettos they never need see, except in the picture magazines, on television or when behind a mop, broom or tray. He was urbane, witty and fake-informative.

His Lotus was known over most of the South Side and although he had to put on its hardtop so as not to muss the hair or wigs of his dates, he enjoyed it very much, as much as any part of his cover. He cultivated the police and politicians and the members of his board of directors. Freeman was constantly pointed out as an example of what a Negro could accomplish if he tried hard enough. He was considered an example of Negro progress and no one concerned themselves with the increasing unemployment in the ghetto, the fact that Negroes continued to fall behind in national economic statistics. Freeman was a good salve for the nonexistent conscience of the white man, that vacuum the editorials spoke of as having been aroused by the "Negro Revolt." Freeman told them what they wanted to hear and was just argumentative enough in cocktail parties to have whites refer to him as "militant, but responsible." Freeman was the best Tom in town. His cover was as good as it ever figured to be and would probably not be blown before he could get his program under way. It was time to begin. He gathered his lieutenants at his apartment, plus a few other members of the Cobras, including Pretty Willie du Bois.

"This summer is the scene, but we need a few things first; most of all bread. We been building up the war chest with what we been stealing, plus whatever we make peddling shit in New York, but we don't have near enough. Sugar Hips, how we stand?"

"We got a balance of $8432.86."

"Right. That ain't enough for what we have to do, so we have to get more. We take it from whitey and we get it from where he keeps it." Freeman spread plans on his cocktail table. "These are the floor plans for the bank in the shopping center on 115th and Halsted. We ought to be able to get a bit more than a hundred thousand dollars. They have a closed-circuit TV and automatic cameras, plus a very sophisticated alarm system. When they touch it off, it alerts the nearest precinct station, but makes no noise.

"There are only two guards, one on the floor, the other on a balcony above, behind one-way, bulletproof glass, with ports for firing to the floor below, but we hit the bank when it's crowded and he won't be able to fire for fear of hitting some innocent bystander. The only tight moment is when you move out and he might get a clear shot as you go through the door, but you'll move to the door with a couple of people as a shield, then shove them back in and make it. He'll be able to hear you up there and make it clear that if he starts firing at any time, you start wasting the crowd.

"It's a short hop to the Negro section in Princeton Park and since it's all middle-class nice, the cops are not likely to search it. That's where we hide out, in the house of Pretty Willie's mother, who's in New Orleans for the Mardi Gras. Besides, they're not going to be looking for niggers, anyway, but for white men."

They looked at him with curiosity. He drained his bottle of Carlsberg before he spoke.

"Pretty Willie leads it. He takes Red Beans, Benny Rooster, Po' Monty and Pussy Head."

They looked at one another and smiled, except Pretty Willie. Freeman had named the lightest-colored members of the Cobras.

"No, goddamnit; I ain't white, I'm a nigger," said Willie.

"Sure, baby, we know that, but that day whitey is going to think you're white. They'll be looking for everybody except us. Niggers don't rob banks, man, you know that. With a gun in your hand, telling Mr. Charlie what to do, to give you his money, why, man, you got to be white," said Dean.

"Look, baby, you know we need the bread and you know none of the rest of us can do it. They must not have more than twenty niggers with accounts there and if five walk in at the same time, they're going to be suspicious. You the only one in the gang can do it because, although your soul is black, your skin is white," added Scott.

"No!" said Willie.

"Man," said Stud. "Don't you see how beautiful it is? I mean, you're turning him around. We all know you a nigger and so does whitey when you on the block with your skinny-brim hat, hangin' out with the cats. He never treat you any different from the rest of us, 'cause you ain't black? Hell no, he gives you a harder time. Now, you got a chance to turn it around."

"No."

Dean spoke up. "Turk, give us a chance to talk about it. Willie, you don't have to do it if you don't want to." He looked at Freeman for confirmation. Freeman nodded. "And, nobody going to put you down if you don't." He swept the room with hard eyes. "We all know you hung-up 'bout not being black, just like some hung-up 'cause they is black. So come on down to the poolroom and we talk about it a little. You don't want to do it, you don't do it and we do it some other way. OK, Turk?" Freeman nodded again. "Crazy, let's split. Stud, you go see your ol' lady, 'cause you might get bugged and want to get physical and there ain't going to be no shit like that, dig. 'Sides, I ain't sure you could whip Pretty Willie, anyway."

They all laughed and relaxed, including Willie and Stud. They were both good enough not to have to worry about the difference. They finished the beer, took the bottles into the kitchen and filed out.

Three days later Freeman received a call from Dean.

"Turk, it all right. Pretty Willie do it. Funny thing, he kind of happy 'bout it now. Never seen the cat smile so much."

"OK, come on by tonight. We'll need about two weeks to get it down pat and it will have to be before the weather turns good. The worse, the better."

It only took them ten days of coaching to get the details right, but a warm-air mass moved up from the Gulf and turned Chicago into a muddy, messy swamp of slush and snow that would freeze at night in the grotesque shapes that had been molded by tires during the day. They waited a week before the snow came again and then the temperature dropped swiftly one moonless night, hovering around zero and turning the icy streets into a glassy surface that sent cars spinning if braked too suddenly. The sky was a slate gray the next morning, seeming to hover just above the rooftops, heavy and leaden, threatening to fall on the ugly city below.

They left for the shopping center at noon, by separate routes, and by that time the temperature had risen and a fine wind-blown snow slanted to cover the icy streets. Freeman drove a Mini-Minor with Scandinavian ice tires on the front wheels, the front-wheel drive gripping the ice firmly. It was modified to serve as a delivery truck for a small dry cleaner's, whose owner ate lunch at home and napped afterward. They had timed him and he never returned to work before three in the afternoon. They had stolen the car and changed the front tires. Freeman drove alone into the big parking lot not more than a hundred yards from the bank. The others arrived in a Willys station wagon, its four-wheel drive giving it stability on the icy streets. Freeman watched as they approached the bank separately. He could see into the bank through the big glass doors. There were about three dozen people inside, other than the employees. Not many, but enough.

He watched Pretty Willie walk in last and without hesitation pull his gun. Mouths opened to scream and shout, but no sound reached Freeman outside. They had been lucky and one of the guards was at lunch. The other reached for his gun and Willie dropped him with a bullet in the thigh. Monty was the closest to the guard; he kicked his gun away and then kicked him in the head until he lay quiet. Two of the others vaulted the cashier's counter and began stuffing money into canvas laundry bags. Willie watched the ports above for the sign of a gun barrel, unaware that the guard was absent. No one else moved. First Pussy Head, then Rooster moved from around the counter, bags full of money in each hand. Freeman started the car and wheeled swiftly in front of the bank, the back of the small truck toward the doors. They moved out of the bank and into the truck and Freeman drove off quickly. Dean, across the street and using the hood of the Willys wagon as a gun rest, fired a deer rifle with scope sights high into the glass doors, pinning the occupants to the floor. He emptied the chamber and got into the truck, following the Mini north on Halsted. Freeman drove to Ninety-fifth and turned east, coming to rest in front of Willie's house after zigzagging to it from five blocks away. They moved swiftly into the house with the money and he drove away and left the car in a residential neighborhood and was picked up by Stud Davis in another car. They had left the stolen Mini in a white neighborhood.

In fifteen minutes Freeman was home sipping twelve-year-old scotch, waiting for the bathtub to fill with very hot water.

Later that evening he watched the news on television and heard the announcer describe the daring daylight robbery of the bank. They were all listed as Caucasian in the police description of the bandits. Freeman smiled. A nigger with a gun in a bank with a lot of money had to be white because niggers snatched purses and rolled drunks—any cop could tell you that—they just didn't rob banks.

Freeman now had an army and a treasury. He needed an arsenal and he knew where he could get that. Then he could start messing with white folks.


Spring came early as if in apology for the fierce winter, the sun bright in pale blue skies, fat white clouds floating overhead, the ore boats moving lazily to the steel mills at the lake's southern tip. The buds burst, the city turned green, and the grime did not seem so noticeable, the noise of the El not so annoying, the stench of the fumes from the buses not so poisonous. For a few days in spring and fall Chicago seems almost fit for human habitation.

Baseballs, footballs, basketballs filled the air in the ghetto, the spherical symbols of a possible escape from the ghetto cage. The junkies stood and sat in the warm sun, their dope-filled blood moving sluggishly in their veins, the ugly world taking on a warm glow, everything soft and pretty prior to their moving through the streets at night looking for loot to support their habit. The winos drank their sweet wine beneath the El tracks, their hoarse voices rising with laughter as the sweet alcohol filled them; the unemployed who still stubbornly hoped were in the Loop and at the factories on the periphery of the city looking for jobs that did not exist; their more realistic black brothers stood and joked in front of the poolrooms, sat in front of countless TV sets in countless bars or drank beer from quart bottles in paper bags. The squad cars moved slowly through the ghetto, stopping here and there to collect their graft. Whores arose, dressed and moved into the unfamiliar sunlight toward a restaurant and late afternoon breakfast. Whites moved through the ghetto like maggots on a carcass: cops, social workers, schoolteachers, bill collectors, the supervisors and collectors of the syndicate, the owners of taverns, furniture stores, currency exchanges, television stores. The ghetto moved into the streets—from the hovels where they had huddled during the winter—where they would stay until the Chicago cold forced them to return to their small smelly rooms for another winter.

They moved through Washington Park on a cool moonless night toward the big National Guard Armory that stood on Cottage Grove Avenue on the Park side. Freeman led two strike teams of five each, Stud Davis in charge of one, Pretty Willie heading the second, Dean as Freeman's second-in-command. There was a wire fence separating the armory from the park. They scaled the fence easily. Freeman motioned to Stud, and Davis and three others moved silently toward the bored guard. There would be two guards walking the armory perimeter and four more inside for relief. They were regular army, their commander a master sergeant who drove home to Winnetka along the outer drive each night. The first heard nothing, right up until the time he was grabbed from behind and borne to the ground by Stud. The second turned his head before he was hit, but had no time to yell. The rest were simply locked in the guardroom, bound and gagged after being confronted by the silent men with their faces covered by nylon stockings.

Freeman forced the lock on the room holding the arms. He had chosen this armory because it was a white unit in the segregated Illinois guard and they figured to have more modern equipment than in either of the Negro armories. He found that they were in luck and in addition to M-1s there were grease guns, pistols, M-14 and M-16 rifles and several thousand rounds of ammunition for the weapons. He moved quickly through the storeroom, selecting the weapons they would use: grease guns, Colt .45 automatics and ammunition for both, fragmentation, smoke and tear-gas grenades, grenade launchers, gas masks, four Springfield .03 sniper rifles with scopes and ammo for them, eight bazookas and rockets.

He was disappointed to find no plastic explosives, only TNT and detonators, but it was better than nothing.

He moved through the room, indicating what should be moved into the yard outside the armory. He chose a grease gun, slipped a full magazine into it, jacked a round into the chamber and slipped the safety on. He waited outside, the gun at the ready while his men moved the arms and ammunition. The empty green and white CTA bus blinked its lights two blocks away and he motioned to Pretty Willie to open the gates on the Cottage Grove side of the building.

The bus was driven by a Cobra. It took less than twenty minutes to load the bus and since a CTA garage was less than three blocks south of the armory on Cottage Grove, no one thought it strange to see an empty bus on the street. Within an hour, the arms and ammunition were cached and Freeman was ready. He need only wait for the hot, humid summer and an arrogant, head-whipping cop to spark the riots. It was like waiting for the sun to shine in the Sahara Desert. Freeman did not think that there would be much searching of the ghetto for the arms because niggers didn't steal government property and defy the FBI any more than they robbed banks.

# 13

---

Spring ended abruptly. A hot, moist air mass moved up from the Gulf of Mexico across the plains and into Chicago, smothering the city and turning the night into a furnace, the brick buildings radiating the heat collected from the sun during the day. Life in the ghetto moved outside, onto the doorsteps of the houses, into the air-conditioned bars and the cinemas that sold cool air and Doris Daydreams. On the South Side there was Washington Park, and families moved at night into its cool greenness, sleeping on blankets under the stars until the first rays of sun, returning to their stifling rooms to snatch a few more minutes of sleep before meeting the hot, humid day. Beer, watermelon, ice cream, anything cool, but there was no way to leave the engulfing heat. The city lay gasping like a big beast. Tempers shortened, and the ghetto lay like a bomb waiting to explode.

Freeman thought that it would begin on the West Side, but it began on the South Side, not far from his home.

A cop killed a fifteen-year-old boy beneath the El tracks near Fiftieth Street. A group of them had been drinking beer when the cop ordered them on; someone threw a brick and the policeman drew his gun. He claimed that the boy advanced with a knife, others disputed his claim, but for the neighborhood the dispute became irrelevant. The word of the shooting spread and the streets filled with people. The wails of sirens sounded as riot-trained police sped to the area.

Freeman's phone rang.

"Turk, this is Sugar. Daddy say to tell you it look like it's going to begin. They got people in the street."

"Right. Where are you?"

"In the poolroom."

"Stay there until you hear from me. I'll call back in about an hour."

He called his office and told the girl on night duty to alert his street workers and said that he would call again within the hour. He got into his car and headed for Fifty-first Street.

He walked up to a squadrol and spoke to a cop he had known in high school. "Hi, Bill, how does it look?"

"Hey, Dan. Not too good. Young cop panicked and burned a kid and people are bugged. You know what happens when you have this kind of heat for this long; anything will touch them off. We got cops moving around in there now, spades in plain clothes telling them to cool it and go home. It's the kids I'm worried about. If they get started, it could spread."

"Anything I can do to help?"

"You know some of the kids around here, don't you? Tell me you pretty tight with the Cobras."

"Yeah, I know them."

"Well, one of your street workers is in there already. It wouldn't hurt if you went in, too. But get the hell out if it looks bad. We don't need any heroes."

"You think it might get bad?"

"I hope not, but I think so. These people wouldn't spend ten minutes in a picket line, but they'd fight all night. We've been lucky so far, but you know Chicago, if it really goes it will make those other riots look like picnics."

"OK, Bill, I'll see what I can do."

"Get the hell out of there if they start raising hell. And check back with me every now and then. Dawson is in charge there. You know him."

"Right. Take it easy, man."

"I just hope the brothers take it easy. Rioting won't help things any."

"The picket lines don't seem to have helped much, either."

"Yeah, and that's the bitch of it."

Freeman walked down Indiana Avenue. People milled about in the streets. The jitneys had stopped making their runs up and down the streets and were either elsewhere or parked on side streets. He had noticed signs already in the windows indicating which stores were Negro owned.

Plainclothes police moved through the crowds, softly urging the people to return to their homes. Here and there men harangued knots of listeners about whitey and police brutality. The police were particularly nervous about rioting on the South Side because it was not a solid ghetto; there were whites in the big housing development near the hospital on Thirty-first Street which had replaced the slums there as part of urban renewal and it was separated from the Negroes by only the broadness of South Park Boulevard. There were whites a short distance away in Hyde Park. Rioting would not be easy to contain and might entail more than just the burning of stores and buildings.

Freeman moved through the crowds, listening and trying to gauge their mood. There was a chance that they might cool off and return to their homes. There was also a chance that they might explode any minute. He spotted Stud Davis and walked toward him.

"Hey, Stud, what's happening?"

"Nothing shakin', man." They walked out into the street away from the crowds.

"You been to the poolroom?"

"Yeah. Daddy, Hips and Pretty Willie's there."

"Where are the rest?"

"Out in the street, like the plan."

"You think they'll blow?"

"Yeah, and I don't even think we'll have to start it. Some of the younger kids are ready to start raising hell. If a cop start leaning on somebody, it's gonna blow, but the fuzz been real cool so far."

"You seen my street worker?"

"Perkins? Yeah, he was around here a few minutes ago; I think he's in the next block. I think he kinda scared."

"Yeah? Well, so am I. Cool it."

He walked down the block, feeling the tension in the air, the look of expectancy everywhere, on the faces of the people, the children, the cops. The cops were seasoned veterans, no rookies, and they would not act hastily; they had kept the white cops on the periphery.

Freeman turned west and then south and walked back to Fifty-first Street. The cops had ordered the bars and liquor stores closed. The whites who owned businesses had faded into the night and the only white faces on the street were those of the police. Freeman was told to move on several times by nervous cops and had to show his identification twice as he strolled down the street toward the east, watching the police in riot helmets and the angry faces of the crowd. Everyone waited for something to happen. Television crews moved here and there with hand-held cameras and cameras mounted on the roof of their equipment trucks, their bright lights giving a harsh glare and casting grotesque shadows. The blue lights on top of the squad cars revolved and winked every few yards. Gas masks were distributed and boxes of tear-gas canisters opened. Ambulances and paddy wagons stood at the ready. Cops spoke busily into their car radios and handy-talkies. Everywhere they clutched their nightsticks tightly like magic wands which would give them strength, beauty and power.

The smells were still there; barbecue, fried chicken, fried shrimps, greens, beans and corn bread. But the sounds of the ghetto were not there: the jukeboxes silent and no soul music from inside the bars and restaurants, barbecue joints or from the loudspeakers hung outside the record store; none of the laughter, shouts to friends, the teasing arguments or quick, staccato bursts of angry profanity, no whistling, humming or someone singing to themselves. The clatter of the El was present as it moved south toward Englewood or Jackson Park stations, or north to Howard Street, but otherwise there were alien sounds: the crackle of the police radios and handy-talkies, the disembodied voices over bullhorns, the sullen murmur of the milling crowds and the keening songs of hate by the street speakers. The air hung hot and heavy and there was no hint of a sudden rain to break the heat wave.

Freeman turned north on Indiana Avenue for the second time that night and approached Perkins, his street worker, who was talking to Detective Sergeant Pete Dawson.

"Hey, Dawson, Perk. How do things look?"

"Not good," said Dawson. "It could blow any minute, or maybe not. We hope we can keep it sealed off if it does go. We're keeping the white cops out of here for now. The cat that wasted the kid was ofay. He didn't have any choice, the kid came at him with a knife. It was self-defense." He sounded as if he were trying to convince himself more than Freeman and Perkins. They all knew that the cop had emptied his gun and missed only once. Standard procedure was to try and drop an assailant with a shot in the thigh or leg. Dawson shook his head. "The cop shouldn't have gone into that dark alley alone. He's new down here; he's used to having people respect the uniform.

"We keep them moving, but as soon as we break up one group, another forms in the next block. This heat is a bitch, maybe they'll run out of energy and go home." They looked at one another. They all knew that it was hotter in those buildings than in the street.

"Anything we can do, Dawson, to help?"

"Just what you been doing. Tell the kids to cool it, they'll listen to you and Perk. I don't think there will be any head whippin'; the cops in here have orders and they're all pretty cool. Tough, but cool and the people here know how far they can push them."

Freeman turned to Perkins. "How does it look to you, Perk? Kids nervous?"

"Yeah, everybody but the Cobras. They seem to take the whole thing as some kind of joke. They're sitting around in small groups coolin' it. Stud Davis is on the block, the other leaders seem to be shootin' pool."

"They're on junk," said Dawson. "Junkies don't care about this kind of scene."

"What about the others, Perk?"

"Well, the Bearcats are out in force, but I don't think they'll start anything, although they might join in if something starts. But the Apaches might start trouble, they'd like to take over from the Cobras. And I've seen a few Comanches around. Not many though, since they sealed off the area."

"OK, Perk. First, get down to the drugstore and phone the office. Get the rest of the street workers down here. Then keep moving around. Keep in close touch with the Apaches, with their leaders, tell them to cool it. I'll be around." He turned to Dawson. "Take it easy, baby."

"Yeah, man, nothing else to do." He walked off down the street.

Freeman moved among them, talking to them, listening sympathetically to their angry protests. He soothed them and told them to go home, that rioting would do no one any good and he did not shuck. You either work at a cover, or forget it. And he did not feel that he would have to do anything to start the thing; he knew if not tonight, there would be some other night like this one. Whitey was stupid and stubborn about Negroes. He would not believe that Negroes would not continue to passively accept the pushing around that whites had come to think of as their birthright. The white cops on Fifty-first Street, he knew, felt that all they had to do was to charge the people here, make enough arrests of the ringleaders, bloody enough heads, a bit of tear gas, guns fired overhead and if need be, shoot a few niggers and they would tuck their tails between their legs and become silent and invisible once more. They would not believe that things had changed and that these people had had enough.

They listened to Freeman because they trusted him, although they did not agree with what he was saying that night because they were too angry and frustrated. They remembered now the waiting in vain for jobs that never materialized; the long humiliating lines to sign the papers thrust at them by arrogant clerks at the unemployment compensation office; the slights and insults of the social workers; the welfare raids on their women's rooms in the middle of the night in an effort to catch a man there. The streets seemed hotter, dirtier, uglier, smellier than they had ever been and no one seemed to care. But tonight they cared, tonight these people were not invisible, tonight whitey knew they existed and there were among them those who wanted whitey to remember this night for years to come.

A bit after midnight they began to cool down, some to drift to their small, hot rooms for a beer and the late show on TV. The Negro cops in their midst sensed the change with relief. And then it happened.

It was the dogs. The truck with the four dogs and their handlers was to have been parked outside the area, to be used only on orders from the commander of the riot task force, but someone made a mistake and the truck stopped at the intersection of Fifty-first and Indiana Avenue. The commander had left his command post there to check the roadblock at South Park. One of the dog handlers approached a captain of police.

"Hello, Captain. We just brought the dogs down. You want us to go in?"

"Well, the commandant and the second-in-command aren't here right now. I dunno."

"How are things so far?"

"Well, they got the colored cops in there. Been in for a few hours. Been kinda tense, but nothing big so far. They're trying to use persuasion." His mouth twisted at the word. "Things have sure changed since I joined the force. All this scientific crap the new commissioner put in. Hell, we can't fart if a computer don't say so. Send three squads of big Irish cops in there, a little tear gas and we can all go home and have a beer."

"Maybe they can use us in there, Captain. These dogs will move 'em. Never seen it to fail."

"Yeah, one thing a nigger is scared of, it's a dog. Go ahead in, but you better report to Dawson, he's a shine detective lieutenant. Thinks he's hell on wheels because he's got some college. You don't report to him, he'll be complainin' to the chief."

"I'm special duty, attached to headquarters downtown. I don't have to worry about no jig lieutenants!" He walked away to the van, a big man who carried his vast belly well, like a pro tackle in his last years, using his bulk and experience to add a few more seasons toward his pension. He motioned to the others and they opened the van carefully, first talking to the dogs to calm them and then in fierce command voices ordering them one by one to the pavement to attach the leashes and remove the muzzles. There were three dark Alsatians and a Doberman. The other cops watched them with interest, the Negro police with flat expressions that said nothing.

The big cop in charge of the detail checked to see that they were ready and adjusted his riot helmet, then drew his club. They advanced across the intersection four abreast and north into Indiana Avenue. It was very quiet now, the eyes of the cops on the dogs and the noise of an El going south from the station a short distance away echoed loudly through the streets. They moved down the street the short distance in which the shops curled briefly around the corner before stopping abruptly where the residential section of the block began. The people on the porches and steps of the buildings saw them first, the others in the streets turned at their shouts.

"They bringing dogs in! Dogs! They bringin' dogs in!"

The cry was picked up and traveled quickly down the block. The cops continued to advance slowly, four abreast, the dogs straining on their leashes.

"Ofay cops with dogs!"

"What the hell they think this is, Alabama?

"When they going to get the cattle prods and bull whips?"

Some of the people on the steps of the buildings flanking the street disappeared into the hallway, making their way to the garbage cans on the back porches, searching them for bottles, going into the backyards and alleys to look for bricks. The people in the street moved back slowly before the advancing four.

"Git them motherfuckers! This ain't Birmingham, no damn dogs here! Git 'em!"

The first bottle came from a porch, then another from a window on the second floor of a building. They shattered close to the four cops and their straining, snarling dogs. At a signal from the big cop they advanced a few yards at a run, scattering the people in the street before them.

"All right, get back, you people, break it up, go on home now. Move it." A volley of bricks and bottles answered him.

One young black boy stood silently on the sidewalk, not moving. The cop opposite him moved toward him and the Doberman started tearing at his pants leg. The cop ordered the dog off and the boy moved away, but slowly, a look of contempt on his face as he looked the cop in the eye. He had never taken his eyes off the face of the policeman, even as the dog lunged at him. He moved away now, watching the cop with that look, his right pants leg in tatters. The people moved back into the street as the four moved past and they were surrounded now, with a space between them and the black, angry faces that retreated before them, the black faces that followed to their rear.

It was not according to the book. There should be cops to their rear to ensure that the cleared streets remained so, but they were in now and the big cop was stubborn and unafraid. He moved on, holding the big dog easily, his club at the ready, ignoring the missiles thrown at him. If they moved within the proscribed distance, he would order the dog to attack. He moved ahead, staring at them steadily from beneath the visor of his riot helmet, ignoring the shouts, insults, bricks and bottles.

Suddenly someone thrust himself through the crowd and he had to order the dog to relax as he recognized the shield of a sergeant of detectives.

"What the hell are you doing in here with those damn dogs?" shouted Dawson.

"I'm doing my job, that's what," the big cop retorted hotly. "I'm trying to help you. Whose side you on, anyway?"

"Get those dogs out of here right now! Don't you know what dogs mean to these people?"

"The captain told me to bring them in," he responded stubbornly.

"Well, I'm telling you to get them out. I'm in charge here. Where the hell is the chief? He said no dogs."

"I don't know where the chief is and I got my orders."

Dawson drew his pistol from his belt holder. "If you don't move them, you're going to have some dead dogs on your hands." He moved back and aimed at the animal. Four other Negro detectives had appeared, they drew their weapons also.

The big cop looked at them with hate. "OK, we're goin', but you'll hear from headquarters about this. Pullin' a gun on a brother officer!"

Dawson looked at him and said softly: "You're not my brother, buddy." He turned to the crowd as the uniformed police turned about and headed south toward Fifty-first Street with their dogs. "It's OK now, the dogs are leaving, they're going back. Cool it, now. Go on home." But it was too late and Dawson sensed it. The bottles continued to fly, the voices loud in rage.

"They brought the dogs in, just like in Birmingham. It'll be the fire hoses and cattle prods next. They don't give a shit. It the same damn thing anywhere if you black."

"One of the dogs bit a child. A three-year-old girl. She bleeding something awful. They got her in the ambulance and won't let her mother near her! The bastards!"

The word spread quickly about the dogs and hundreds of people converged on the street between Fifty-first and Fiftieth. Dawson and his men moved among them, the crowd jostling some and occasionally they had to strike back. Reluctantly, Dawson fired a red flare, the signal to rendezvous prior to pulling out. He had his men move the crowd back by force, creating a circle twenty feet in diameter.

"Dan, we're moving back as soon as all my men are here. We'll probably have to move the uniformed cops in now. I don't know if we can snuff it out, but we'll have to charge them. Talking's no good anymore. The dogs finished that."

"I can't leave without Perkins, Daws. It's all right, you're not responsible. I think it will be OK for another few minutes, as long as they don't mistake me for a cop." He saw Perkins move quickly into the circle, his face drawn and worried.

"Shit, Dan, they were going home, they were going home. It was going to be fine until they brought them dogs in. It was going to be just fine." He fought back the tears, his face full of exhaustion.

They formed a diamond pattern and forced their way back down the block, striking out when they had to, taking no joy in it. They would have to crack a lot of heads tonight, they knew, and except for the sadists and power hungry among them, they took no pride in attacking their own people.

Finally, they made it to the barricades on the corner and moved through them. The jeering crowd stopped a short distance away, filling the street. The detectives slumped against police cars and vans, some sat on curbs, perspiration dripping from their faces, drenching their clothes. The police stirred nervously, fingering their weapons, their boredom gone. Dawson strode to his car and yanked the microphone from the dash.

"Baker four to Baker one, Baker four to Baker one. Come in Baker one. Over."

"This is Baker one, Baker four. This is Baker one, Baker four. I read you. Over."

"Better get back here, Chief. Looks like it's gonna be bad. Over."

"What happened? I thought things were quieting down. Over."

"They were. It was almost finished, then they brought the dogs in. You know what they think about the dogs. Over." He looked very tired. Someone handed him a cup of coffee in a paper cup.

There was a pause and the radio hummed. "OK, Pete, hold on. I'll be right there. You at the CP? Over."

"Yeah, Chief. You better hurry. Over."

"Right. We're on the way now. Out." Dawson could hear the scream of the siren approaching from the east. He looked up at the man who had handed him the coffee. "Well, Dan, we did what we could."

"Yeah, Daws." Dawson looked over the barricades at the angry mob. He knew many of them; he had lived for years within blocks of here. He knew their anger and their pain, but there was nothing he could do. He was a cop. He would have a very busy night.

"You know, Dan, they were going home. Another hour and you could have been in the Boulevard Lounge tastin' and those people at home. Now look at it. This could be the worst yet. I've never seen them like that before. Why did they bring those dogs in? Why, man? Don't they know how they feel about dogs? How come they so stupid? Everything was cool and they had to mess it up. Why do they always mess it up?"

"I don't know, Daws, but they always do."

# 14

The chief's car screeched into the intersection. Dawson walked slowly to the car and stood talking intently to the chief.

He turned and waved Freeman to the command post. "Chief, this is Dan Freeman."

"Oh, yes, you're with the foundation, aren't you? Been doing a fine job, I hear. Taken a lot of pressure off our precincts down here. They've been trying the same program, but without much success, over on the West Side. Pete tells me you were in there talking to the teenage gangs. How does it look to you?"

"When it starts, they'll be the most dangerous and the most destructive. They haven't been rumbling and so they have a lot of latent hostility to get rid of. Now they have a chance to hit out and become neighborhood heroes as well. Usually the folks here are afraid of the gangs and hate them, but it might be different after tonight. I don't think the Cobras will be very active, although some of them will probably attach themselves to other gangs."

"Hold on. I thought the Cobras were the worst gang in the city." The chief nodded at Dawson.

"They were, Chief." Dawson shook his head and said one word: "Junk." The chief nodded.

"I think most of the trouble will come from the Apaches. They want to take over the reputation of the Cobras around here. There are a couple of smaller gangs who will join in and there are some of the Comanches in there from the near West Side, from the low-cost housing project on the other side of the Dan Ryan Expressway.

"The Apaches will do the most damage, though. They won't be afraid of anything that moves and getting shot, beaten or arrested they consider a badge of honor. They're going to be hard to control. And some of the older men who have been out of work for a long time will probably join in. There are guns in there, too. Your men will have to watch out for snipers from the rooftops when they go in. I have my street workers on around-the-clock alert. When you think we can help, Dawson knows how to reach me. But they're not likely to listen to any of us now; not since the dogs."

The chief winced. "Thanks, Mr. Freeman. Can one of my men drop you anywhere?"

"No thanks, my car is not far from here. Good luck. See you later, Daws."

"Yeah, Freebee. Easy."

Freeman drove his car away and parked it in Washington Park, then walked back to watch. It wouldn't be long before they went for the stores on Fifty-first and they would probably infiltrate the lines through the alleyways when the police moved into the neighborhood.

But they had already started on Forty-seventh Street. The word about the dogs had spread quickly throughout the cordoned-off quadrangle and they had burst into Forty-seventh Street before the cops there, relaxing because of the reports that things were quieting down, knew that the mood had changed. They moved close to the street through the darkened alleys, then burst out of alleys in several places. Some were caught and arrested, others beaten, but more and more poured into the street.

They went for the pawnshops first, smashing the windows and grabbing whatever they could from the inside until cops approached and then scrambled further down the street. By now there were hundreds in the streets, rampaging, smashing and finally burning and south of Forty-seventh, when the cops were ordered inside the quadrangle, they burst into Fifty-first as well.

They went to the blood-sucking stores as steel filings to a magnet: the pawnshops that contained their few prized possessions, pawned for a fix, a bottle, money to hit a number, to impress a girlfriend, for a wedding, medicine, an abortion. They hit the furniture stores that made more money in interest by reselling the same set of jerry-built furniture to people who could not keep up the payments than if they had sold the junk outright. They hit the supermarkets and liquor stores and then any store that was owned by whites. They would break in the windows and scramble inside, break the lock on the rear door and begin to haul stuff out through the back. When the cops arrived they would leave and move on to the next place being looted.

Freeman watched them on Fifty-first, strolling down the raging street. Once a cop swung at him with a club, he dodged the first blow and flashed his badge and ID, but thought that he might have to defend himself. The white cops were lashing out at anything black, in terror and hate.

A small boy struggled down the street with a small Japanese portable television set. A man went by with a stack of six hats on his head, several ties draped around his neck and a case of bonded bourbon in his arms. A large fat woman waddled down the street with two large hams in each arm. Too slow, she was intercepted and clubbed down by a cop. Three boys in their teens fought savagely with two cops. One of the cops went to his knees and when he reached for his gun, the three disappeared through a broken store window and out into the alley to its rear.

The cops grabbed, clubbed, handcuffed and arrested. The police vans moved out full of men, women and children, many of them bloody. Firemen tried to uncoil a hose to put out a fire in a furniture store and were driven away by a group of teenagers. Everywhere there were angry shouts.

"Burn, baby, burn!"

"Get whitey!"

"Black power!"

A cop was hit in the face with a brick and helped to an ambulance by two others, blood streaming freely onto his dark blue uniform. A boy, running, slipped on broken glass and four cops were upon him, beating and poking savagely at his groin with their night sticks. He screamed and thrashed in pain and they dragged him, bloody and still screaming, to a paddy wagon.

Smoke licked up toward the heavy, humid sky. The police shouted, men, women and children shouted and screamed in anger, hate and pain. One large boy of about nineteen fought a cop, knocked him to the ground with a swinging right hand, then taking his club, beat him while on the ground; then, dashing away, he was shot only two steps from the sanctuary of the dark alley. He lay on the sidewalk moving feebly while the cops carried his victim to an ambulance.

A police car was overturned and set afire, others had their tires slashed. The army of occupation was being attacked everywhere, and since better equipped, having the better of it. But the police took their casualties from bricks, bottles, baseball bats and fists. Sporadic firing broke out inside and Freeman saw two cops brought back to the street, wounded from sniper's fire.

The violence spread, to Fifty-fifth to the south, Forty-third to the north, a section of Halsted Street on the West Side. Everywhere the pattern was the same, break, loot, burn and run. Hurt the cops if you could, run if you couldn't. Take anything of value, stash it at home and then move back into the streets for more. Smash any store owned by whitey; he takes your bread to the suburbs where you can't live, he cheats you, overcharges you, insults you and your women, he hates and despises you. Hit him where it will hurt most: in his pocketbook.

Stores were stripped, then set ablaze. Everywhere people moved, laden with loot. The cops, both white and black, exhausted, frustrated, no longer feared or in control, struck out whenever they cornered someone. Ghetto cops operate in a state of near paranoia and now they had been pushed over the line. Their protection, their status, their power is based on fear and now these people no longer feared them and the status quo had to be resumed. Gunfire increased, even people who surrendered when challenged were beaten to the ground and dragged to the ever-waiting vans. There were no longer any efforts to protect property, only efforts to restore law and order at any cost. The clubs were transferred to left hands and everywhere Freeman looked there were cops on the prowl with drawn guns. People lay sprawled in the streets and sidewalks and cops fired at every fleeting shadow.

Freeman moved down the middle of the street, slowly and smiling, his hands a bit from his sides to show the cops he carried no loot and had no weapons. It was no place now for a black man not in uniform. He thought it would be a hell of a time for him to die, walking innocently down this street, shot by a scared, hate-filled cop. It would be poetic justice, considering what he planned, and he smiled at the thought. He caught the acrid smell of tear gas, borne from inside by a brief, weak breeze. Smoke filled the street, there was broken glass everywhere, overturned cars, empty cartridge cases, discarded loot, an abandoned pair of handcuffs, a pair of nylon stockings lying in a pool of congealing blood. A puppy cowered beneath a car, whimpering. In the broken window of an electrical appliance store stood a color television console, too large to be carted away, sitting there like a fat, rich dowager on a garbage heap. The rest of the store was littered and empty of its wares. The big set was turned on and Freeman could see the rioting filmed live and in color. It was a bit out of focus and he walked over and adjusted a dial until it came in sharp and clear. He watched a moment, cops on the screen fired at an unseen sniper on a rooftop, the deep voice of the narrator sounding as if he were commenting on a high-budget Hollywood film about the Normandy invasion. Freeman thought the cops looked more heroic on the television set than there on the streets. He turned and walked away.

He was stopped three times and once he talked calmly and inched closer to an hysterical cop, who waved a pistol in his face. Before Freeman could disarm him, the cop turned to a wall and sobbed into his folded arms, tightly clutching his pistol and club. Freeman waved to another cop and was almost shot until the cop realized Freeman was not threatening a brother officer. They helped the sobbing policeman into an ambulance and Freeman walked on toward the park.

He walked down the middle of the street, past the television cables, cops, cars, cartridge boxes, trucks, television vans, ambulances, equipment and debris. He stopped, facing toward the park a short distance away, listening to the alien sounds. No music, he thought, no good here without the music. He thought of what he would be doing from now on, and of the years during which he had prepared himself. He had known that one day this moment would come. He wished it had not.

He breathed deeply, trying to shut out the foreign smells until he could grasp one which belonged on this street and finally he could. He breathed deeply and savored the smell of barbecue.

He drove to his apartment and phoned Daddy at the poolroom.

"We still here like you say, Turk; been watchin' things on TV. Don't look good."

"It looks worse out there in those streets. Three more days of that and the people ought to be fed up enough with whitey to back us."

"What if they stop before then?"

"That's the chance we have to take, but I don't think they will. Not after tonight. The cops will make sure of that. They're going crazy down there. Tomorrow they'll divide by ten to come up with casualty figures for the press. You heard from Stud?"

"Yeah, he called 'bout fifteen minutes ago. Man, he having a ball. Almost got burned twice and busted half a dozen times, but he still loose and raisin' hell."

"When he calls again tell him to get out of sight and lay low as soon as things get tight in there. They'll be looking for him when things quiet down. How about the others?"

There was a pause.

"They shot Tony, one of the young kids. They took him away in an ambulance. Stud say, so maybe he ain't dead. They only arrest two others. Stud say them young Cobras is a bitch, slippery and mean as hell."

"OK, I'll check the hospitals tomorrow morning about Tony. Look, you cats better not be seen in the street tonight."

"Naw, Turk, we gonna stay here tonight. We got beer and some food, a deck of cards and the TV. When we get tired we can sleep on the tables."

"OK, baby, I'll call again in the morning. If anything important happens, call me. And tell Stud not to stay down there too long. He's no good to us dead or in jail." He hung up and when he had finished soaking in a hot tub, realized that he was ravenously hungry. He ate a mushroom omelet and almost fell asleep before he had finished eating it.

He arose early the next morning and turned on the television set to catch the news while the coffee brewed. The mayor, in a brief statement, said that "early reports indicated that agitators and Communists were responsible for the rioting." The police commissioner called for a return to law and order and hoped that cooler heads might prevail among the more "responsible citizens of the riot-torn area." A prominent University of Chicago professor of sociology stated that the riots indicated "an increasing pattern of sado-masochistic tendencies as an outgrowth of increased urbanization" and that the rioting was "a parallel to the death wish demonstrated by the Jews in Nazi Germany since the rioters could only face eventual repression." Prominent Negro leaders, none of whom had been in the riot area in years in spite of the fact that most lived within walking distance, deplored the riots and advocated nonviolence as the only means of attaining progress for Negroes. A former vice-president said that rioters should be shown no mercy, regardless of color. The governor of Alabama said I told you so. The governor of Illinois announced that the National Guard had been alerted.

Freeman took the morning newspapers from his doorstep and read them over his first cup of coffee. A cartoonist pictured a bearded figure in sunglasses with exaggerated Negroid features, clad in T-shirt, blue jeans and sandals, attacking a figure labeled "Civil Rights," clad in a Brooks Brothers suit, necktie and hat, who looked like a white man colored dark. The editorial called for a return to nonviolent protest, then suggested that nonviolent protest was responsible for the rioting by fostering disrespect for law and order, and ended by predicting that white backlash would negate the great progress thus far achieved in civil rights.

Freeman's Senator Hennington predicted that the rioting would hurt the civil-rights bill presently on the Senate floor. The president said nothing; his press secretary praised the Negroes fighting for the freedom of the Vietnamese. Three prominent authors, two playwrights and four movie stars resigned from civil-rights organizations in protest. A Negro leader requested the installation of sprinklers on fire hydrants, a swimming pool in the West Side ghetto and the hiring of Negro pilots by Trans-World Airlines. Each of the Negro aldermen denounced "hoodlumism, lawlessness and violence" and praised the mayor for his achievements for the Negro population of Chicago. Their statements were identical because they had been written in the mayor's office of public relations.

The House of Representatives Un-American Activities Committee announced that they would hold hearings in Chicago to investigate Communist agitation among the rioters. The *Chicago Tribune* requested the National Guard; the *Daily News* suggested that Negroes prove themselves worthy of full citizenship by becoming model noncitizens first; the *Sun-Times* requested an increase in federal antipoverty funds. *Time-Life* flew in a staff of sixty-three, *Newsweek* a staff of thirty-eight and the *Times* of London authorized a round-trip ticket by Greyhound bus for its New York stringer, to cover the riots.

The television networks thought that riots in the North might replace the now absent police dogs, fire hoses, cattle prods and mounted state troopers of the South in entertainment value. They each dispatched top-flight task forces to cover the rioting in full color. Antonioni announced plans in Rome to do a technicolor movie concerning the riots. It would involve one man's agony in trying to decide whether to throw a brick at the police and the entire movie would take place in a kitchenette apartment. Marcello Mastroianni would play the lead in blackface.

Mr. Stephens, chairman of the board of the foundation, phoned Freeman and asked that he be present at an emergency meeting of the board at 3:30 that afternoon. Freeman ate a large breakfast and drove to the riot area.

# 15

Freeman parked his car outside the cordoned-off riot area and walked through the checkpoint after showing his ID to the cop stationed there. A short distance down the street he found Dawson seated in his patrol car, sipping a cup of coffee, his face drawn with fatigue. Freeman walked over to the car when he waved to him.

"Hey, Freebee, what you doin' in here; don't look like much work for you for awhile."

"Hi, Daws. Come over to check out the scene; got a board meeting this afternoon and they'll want a report."

"OK, hop in, I'm just going to cruise the area."

Freeman seated himself next to Dawson. "Where's Turner?" he asked.

"At a briefing downtown; they couldn't spare both of us. He'll bring me up to date this afternoon when he gets back." He eased the car into the streets, empty except for official vehicles cruising the neighborhood. The word had spread that the cops had become trigger-happy and the people were in their buildings or sitting silently in groups on the porches; few ventured casually into the streets.

"How long since you had some sleep, Daws?"

"Oh, I been catnapping now and then. They talking about bringing in the National Guard. I don't like the idea of seeing military uniforms in here. And the unit they alerted is an all-white outfit, too. That won't help things at all, but they don't trust the colored guard unit. Or many of us spade cops, either; they been acting like we started it instead of putting it down. Man, the colored cops worked harder than anyone here." Dawson fell silent a moment, gazing through the windshield. The groups of people on the porches followed the car sullenly with their eyes. The odor of smoke hung heavy in the air and the police calls from the squad-car radio sounded loud because of the unusually quiet streets.

"You know, Dan, I grew up around here, but I wonder if I really know or understand these people."

"Well," said Freeman, "that badge does put distance between you and the rest."

"Yeah," replied Dawson. "I saw some good friends out in the street last night; not just hoodlums like they say on TV, but some very straight cats, cats with jobs, families, responsibility."

"In a scene like that, everybody can get involved, Daws."

"It was like it was war and I was part of the enemy. Some I can understand, they were always in trouble, but what were the others thinking? It wasn't like they hated me, it was like I was in the way of something important they had to do.

"What good will it do? It's not enough to say they had it tough; they didn't have it any tougher than we did. Without respect for law and order, we might as well be back in the jungle." Dawson parked the car on Fifty-first Street and they stared at a burned-out store, the burn smell heavy in the rapidly warming late-morning air.

"Shit, Daws, the ghetto's always been a jungle. You really think you can treat people like animals and not have them act like animals? You really believe you're just a cop and I'm just a social worker? Man, we're keepers of the zoo. You can't cage a whole race of people without asking for trouble."

"You agree with what they did?" Dawson turned to face Freeman, one arm draped on the steering wheel.

"No, because it won't mean a thing. You watch how the white folks will turn it around. They'll have a flood of people down here running surveys and shit, all designed to find out how to maintain the racial status quo without paying riot dues; how to get the niggers to go back to sleep. Whitey won't get the message because he doesn't want to get it. Things will quiet down and we'll both go back to working for Mr. Charlie—keeping niggers in their place."

The police calls came through the radio with a metallic quality, echoing in the quiet street. The sound of an approaching El grew in the distance.

"I can't buy that, Freebee," said Dawson seriously. "Somebody has to do what we're doing and we're a lot better than most. Don't you think it's better to have a cop who grew up here, who knows the people?" The El stopped at the station just down the street; the people aboard pushed close to the windows to gaze raptly at the ravaged street below.

"Better for whitey. It takes a nigger to catch a nigger."

"The streets have to be safe."

"Whose streets? Were our streets safe for our women when we were kids? Whitey discovered Negro crime when it spilled out of the ghetto and began threatening him. They don't give a damn what we do to one another." Two big cops in full riot gear, carrying three-foot riot sticks, noticed Freeman in the squad car and approached it in case Dawson needed assistance. Dawson waved them away and started the car, moving west toward State Street.

"We have to clean up our own backyard before we can expect whites to help us."

"You come on like *Time* magazine, man. The conditions they force us into cause the crime, then they use the crime to justify the conditions."

"If every Negro worked as hard as you have to get where you are, we wouldn't have a problem."

"Later for that jazz, Daws: run twice as fast to get half as far; whitey sitting there with his hand on the controls of the treadmill laughing his ass off."

"I don't think you really believe that." They had turned into an alley and the backyards were crisscrossed with lines of wash, the back porches crowded with people. One man arose, walked to the railing of his porch and contemptuously spat at the squad car as it slowly moved down the alley. "It's not easy working and going to law school, but in a couple of years I'll have my degree and I think it's worth the extra effort." He waved toward the crowded porches.

"If everyone out there devoted as much energy trying to improve themselves as they did last night burning and looting, they might be where we are."

"Where we are? Where the hell are we? How are we any different from them?"

"You know we're not like them."

"You think we're different because you got a badge and I got a couple of degrees?"

"We gotta be."

"You know what whites call people like you and me in private?"

"What?"

"Niggers!"

"Cool it." He looked at Freeman with an inquiring smile. Freeman, working to control his anger, forced himself to return the smile. "I know you don't really believe that stuff, Dan. You're tired and upset about this scene, just like me."

"Yeah, I guess you're right, Daws. It does bug me to see all that work go down the drain. When things quiet down again, I have to start right from scratch. How long you been on the force now?"

"Almost fifteen years. I can retire with a full pension after twenty. I joined right after I dropped out of school when I got hurt and it finished me for football."

"How come you quit school? Even though you couldn't play anymore, they figured to continue your ride. Public relations for future recruiting."

"Yeah, I know, but I just couldn't stay around after having been the big hero. I had two good seasons, Dan, two very good ones. They were letting freshmen compete in the Big Ten at that time, remember? I made first string as a freshman and even missing two games the next season after I injured my knee, I made all-conference as a sophomore." He paused, remembering.

"You would have been a cinch for All-American if you hadn't missed those two games; even so, you got honorable mention for AP and third string for *Look* magazine."

"That's the hang-up, Dan, everything was so groovy and then, nothing. Man, I couldn't stay around, the crippled ex-football star. I stayed long enough to take final exams so I'd have the credits for the semester and then I just came back to Chicago without even saying goodbye to anyone. The school was straight, though, they paid for the operation on the knee and as soon as it was strong enough to pass the police physical exam, I joined the force and I've been with them ever since."

Freeman asked the next question carefully. "Aren't you about due for a promotion?"

Dawson laughed bitterly. "You trying to put me on, Freebee? You know the quota is full up: one spade captain of uniformed police and one lieutenant of detectives. If either one drops dead, I'm in, otherwise, I'm stuck as a sergeant until one retires. They keep telling me how swinging it is to be a detective sergeant at my age, like they doing me a favor and I had the highest score on the exam when I made sergeant. But, it's not so bad, I could be doing a lot worse."

Freeman thought Dawson was not quite ready yet, but his justified indignation at not having the rank he deserved might be just the wedge he needed to recruit him. And, Freeman thought, the things he would see when the guard came into the neighborhood would not enamor Dawson of white folks. He would bide his time, work on him quietly, plant the seeds and cultivate them over a period of time. Dawson would be a good man. He could take over if they ever blew my cover, Freeman thought. I'll just have to be patient a little bit longer; one day the white man will force him to make a choice, he can't straddle the fence forever. He looked pretty damn good against those dogs last night.

"Daws, why don't we go on down to Mamma Soul Food's on Forty-seventh and eat? I'm starving."

"Good idea, Freebee; some pork chops would knock me out."

They drove through the checkpoint and on to Forty-seventh. They stopped first for a drink in a dark, air-conditioned bar and watched the Cubs playing San Francisco on the television set there. They watched long enough to see Willie Mays double in two runs and then walked the short distance to the small restaurant, ordered and ate in silence, each comfortable in the old friendship and lost in their own private thoughts. When they had finished, Dawson drove Freeman to his car, parked just outside the riot area.

"Easy, Dan, don't let those board members string you out."

"You better hope not, because if they do, I'll join the force and take your job in a couple of years."

Dawson laughed as he drove off. "You might make a pretty good cop; we'd make a good team."

Freeman smiled and waved. Yeah, he thought, we could make a damn good team, but not working for Mr. Charlie.

He drove to his office, not far from the University in the Hyde Park district and on the opposite of Washington Park from the riot area. He entered the paneled reception room, decorated in Danish modern, and smiled at the pretty colored receptionist. "Afternoon, Mr. Freeman. Mr. Stephens wants to see you before the meeting; everybody's shook up today."

"Thanks, honey. I'll try not to lose my cool." He walked down the hall and past Stephens's office into the toilet. As he washed his hands he checked his mask in the mirror for slippage; this was not the time to arouse suspicion. The face that returned his stare in the mirror was sincere, serious, concerned and just a bit worried that it might lose a five-figure salary because the natives had been restless last night. His mask was perfect. He dried his hands, adjusted his tie and walked down the hall to reassure the white folks.

The board members were talking nervously in Stephens's outer office; Stephens's secretary motioned Freeman into the inner office when he arrived.

"Hello, Dan. I'd like a brief report before we convene the meeting. Needless to say, most of the board members are rather agitated about this thing. I understand you were there for most of the worst of it. What happened?"

"Same old thing, the heat was getting to the cops and the people over there and there had been the usual increase in head whippings for the summer-time; then a cop shot a kid and upset a lot of people. They had almost quieted down when they brought dogs in and that was like touching a match to gasoline."

"How was it over there?"

"Pretty bad. Looks as if they might have to call in the guard. I don't think the police can handle it now."

"How about the street gangs?"

"They're in it, but only one, the Apaches, are spearheading anything. No, it's not a hoodlum scene like they say; the whole neighborhood is involved, if not actively, then they support it."

"What do they hope to gain, Dan? This kind of thing could make it worse for them instead of better." Stephens played nervously with a small, bulldog pipe and stared at Freeman intently.

"They don't hope to gain anything. They don't have any hope, any-more, they're convinced nobody gives a damn about them and their prob-lems. They're fed up with being ignored, pushed around and taking crap and now they're kicking back."

"Revenge?"

"No, not revenge, retaliation; there's a subtle but important difference."

For a moment Stephens's face opened and disapproval of Freeman showed there briefly, as if Freeman had been personally responsible for the rioting which now threatened their jobs. Stephens looked down quickly at his desk blotter, the blotter a pale shade of violet held in place with handworked Florentine leather. When he looked up again he had a warm, if somewhat tight, white liberal smile on his face.

"Dan, I've spoken to most of the board members and they're very upset that the money we've spent to prevent exactly what happened last night has been wasted."

"I disagree, Steve. Street-gang activity among the rioters was at an absolute minimum and the Cobras weren't operating at all. The riot-control task force report will substantiate that."

Stephens leaned forward eagerly toward the first sign of hope that morning, like a dog who does not really believe the bone being held out invitingly will be offered.

"That's good news. Do you think the foundation can take any credit for that?" His white liberal glow increased and Freeman fanned the embers.

"Of course. If it hadn't been for the foundation, those kids would have been directly involved and the damage infinitely worse."

"I hope you can confirm this in the meeting, Dan." Stephens licked his lips nervously, hitched his pocket handkerchief and patted it into place as if to be certain his heart still beat beneath it. "There's talk among the board to dissolve the foundation. Burkhardt has been particularly critical. You know what it would mean to have the foundation ended. Jobs like ours don't grow on trees."

Freeman allowed a moment of panic to show in his eyes, then looked out of the window as if to contemplate the horrors of job hunting. He thumbed through his masks and chose one of smiling confidence.

"I picked up a copy of the report of the chief of the riot task force first thing this morning." He opened the slim attaché case he had placed at his feet and offered the report to Stephens like a tranquilizer. He spoke in clipped, somewhat more white-type tones than usual. "It indicates that street-gang activity was a minor factor in the rioting and cites us by name as the major reason for the inactivity of the gangs as units in the rioting." Stephens leafed through the report.

"Good thinking, Dan; this report could prove invaluable. If we can come through this crisis unscathed, we should be a cinch for the Ford grant. And you know that means substantial raises in pay and allowances for both of us. And nationwide prestige as well. Yes, I think this report, plus your own oral presentation today, could turn the trick. We have to increase our budget, not kill the foundation."

"Precisely!" said Freeman.

Stephens decided to fill his pipe; in moments of doubt, his pipe some- how made him feel wiser and more secure. "I talked to the chief on the phone this morning, Dan; he had high praise for your activity last night."

"Perk was there, too; he did a damn good job. I'd like it mentioned in his personnel file."

"Of course, Dan. Draft a statement and I'll endorse it. I think we'd better go into the conference room now. This will be a tough session."

"I don't know," said Freeman. "It's a lot tougher across the park."

Stephens opened the meeting and Freeman gave a brief report.

Burkhardt spoke up: "I might as well be frank about this thing, I'm beginning to have serious doubts about the worth of this foundation. We spend a good deal of money to prevent this very kind of thing and I wonder if we want to pour good money after bad." He wore heavy horn-rimmed glasses too big for his nose and he pushed them back up with a nervous gesture of his right hand.

"The streets aren't safe. What's to prevent some of those hoodlums from coming into Hyde Park to continue their burning and looting? I've sent my wife and children to her mother's in Winnetka and I've loaded my shotgun, deer rifle and pistol!"

Stephens spoke soothingly. "We're all concerned about this kind of thing, Burk, but I don't think it's as bad as all that. Dan here reports that street-gang activity is at a surprising minimum and the commandant of the riot task force confirms it, and he has high praise for Dan here and our foundation.

"Furthermore, the King Cobras, the potentially most dangerous gang in the area, is not functioning in the rioting as a unit and that is the outfit which had our top priority when Dan was brought in."

"Well, that is good news; perhaps the papers have exaggerated a bit. But still, we are less than a mile from the major rioting. What's to prevent it spilling over into our neighborhood?"

Professor Thompson, of the department of sociology and social welfare at the University of Chicago and a foremost expert on juvenile delinquency, spoke: "Well, Burk, we've found that people from lower-income groups, and particularly the culturally deprived and socially disadvantaged, seldom cross what we term natural urban barriers such as the Midway mall, an expressway, large, busy thoroughfare or Washington Park, for instance. The park acts as a natural buffer and I think we need fear little in that sense.

"Fortunately, there are no middle-class areas contiguous on the riot area and there is little chance for the rioters to single out people better off than they as targets of their discontent and frustration."

What you mean, baby, is that there are no white middle-class areas contiguous on the riot area, thought Freeman. The slum portion of the ghetto ends at Sixty-first. But Freeman didn't think they would attack other Negroes, even the black middle class.

"I would tend to agree with Steve, that our organization has performed well beyond the level to be expected. That our activity among the youth of the neighborhood could act as a restraining factor, even in this moment of dramatic social disorganization, is little short of remarkable. In fact, I intend doing a paper concerning our role among the rioters for presentation at the next national convention of the American Society of Sociologists, if Dan would be so kind as to contribute some of his own observations."

What you want, Professor, is for me to write the damn thing for you so you can inject some sociological gobbledygook and call it your own, Freeman thought sourly; but his expression never changed.

The board meeting continued and after Freeman indicated what was planned, once things quieted down in the riot area, Stephens adjourned the meeting. They filed out, stopping to shake Freeman's hand, smiling and calm now, no longer afraid because Freeman was a good nigger, their nigger and he would protect them from the others. Even Burkhardt, who had always been awkwardly brusque with Freeman, smiled, pumped his hand, patted him on the back, chattered small talk at him and suggested they have lunch together one day. That's what they hired me for, thought Freeman, the house slave to keep the dangerous, dumb, nasty field slaves quiet and now that they know that it's only niggers raising hell in their own neighborhood, they feel fine. He watched them from behind his mask, betraying nothing, smiling, saying the right things automatically; then they were gone and he was alone in the room with Stephens.

"Well, Dan, I think that went much better than we had any reason to expect. I'd reminded them all before you arrived that you had predicted trouble of this kind this summer and I think they were pleased at the report regarding juvenile activity last night during the rioting. I think there's a raise in this thing for you."

"What about the street workers?"

"Of course, the street workers, too, but that will have to await the grant from Washington. But, I'm requesting an immediate increase in your salary at the next official board meeting and I can see no opposition on the horizon. How about dinner?"

Freeman couldn't eat with this white man, not after last night. He knew he might lose his cool and blow his cover.

"I don't think so, Steve. I've got a lot of checking to do before the staff meeting tomorrow afternoon. As soon as things settle down over there I'm putting the entire staff of street workers into the area and we'll have to work out a crash program."

"Good idea, Dan. Next week, then." As he turned to leave the conference room Freeman silently handed him his forgotten pipe.

Freeman drove the few blocks to his apartment, took a steak out of the freezer compartment to thaw, put a potato into the oven to bake and made a lettuce-and-tomato salad. He walked into the living room and turned up the air conditioner, then mixed himself a martini. He sat down and sipped the drink slowly, waiting for the steak to thaw, looking at the Javanese Buddha head of black volcanic stone.

He had never thought that he would enjoy what he would do and now that the time had arrived, he knew that he would not enjoy it at all, but that would not change things any. He wondered how many of them would be alive this time next year and he wondered how many more they would kill tonight. The papers had reported three killed, but he had seen five dead the night before on Fifty-first alone—target practice with live ammo and live targets. But then, the bull's-eye of every target he had ever seen had been black.

# 16

Freeman strode through his apartment, tense and restless from the foundation board meeting. His cover was even more secure than ever. He would be free to roam the area, befriend the troops and cops, gathering intelligence as an almost invisible agent, but he would never enjoy deceiving whites. Even in that meeting, one part of him was crying to tell them what he thought and felt; but he couldn't afford to yield to that temptation. There was too much at stake.

He roamed his apartment, turned up the air conditioner and moved to his records. He hesitated in front of the Miles Davis records, then moved to the blues. He chose Muddy Waters, John Lee Hooker, Lightnin' Hopkins, Big Bill Broonzy, and put them on the changer. He stood midway between the speakers and listened to the first few bars of "Hoochie Coochie Man," then walked into the kitchen and filled a Danish teakwood ice container. He mixed a martini of four parts Beefeater gin to one part Noilly Prat vermouth over the rocks, in an old-fashioned glass. He walked to the Saarinen womb chair and sat sipping his drink and listening to the music.

He gazed around the room and there was not a mistake in the cover; it reflected perfectly the superficial, materialistic, white-type, middle-class Freeman. By any contemporary definition, Freeman was a nigger who had made it in white society. He had everything any red-blooded American boy could want; and for a nigger, wow! The apartment gleamed and glistened with chrome, formica, aluminum and steel; shone gently of well-polished wood; bulged with grownup toys: color television, stereo, videotape, exotic carvings and knives. He dressed fashionably and well, read the right books and magazines.

The pay for sellout niggers increases annually, he thought. Yes, the Negro profession is really swinging nowadays, but it looks like I'm going to throw a little shit in the game. When whites find out what they must really know down deep inside, that niggers like me don't really communicate with or control the rest, a whole lot of cats like the fake Freeman will be on the outside looking in. And where will I be after the deal goes down? Can't think about that, got to take it one day at a time, make sure the thing won't end if they get to me. When did it all start, when did I really know that whitey was nowhere for niggers? It would be so easy to sink into the softness of this scene. Let's face it, he thought, I like this shit. I drive a beautiful piece of machinery, drink good whiskey, wear good clothes and have more chicks than I can really handle. It would only take a little lying to myself to think I was really into something; tell myself I'd earned it all in the best Horatio Alger tradition. Put down all the spades too lazy to do what I've done. But whitey helps; he might tell you that you're "different" from the rest and in the next breath remind you you're all the same underneath your manicured fingernails and J. Press suit.

The ghetto had been a refuge in his childhood. He had had no close contact with whites until he entered a high school split almost fifty-fifty, white and black. But it was two schools, as rigidly separated by unspoken rule as if someone had painted signs saying white and colored. Freeman hadn't thought much about the whites; he had his own colored friends.

It happened during the beginning of his second year, just after the war with the black veterans returning from the "war of freedom" bitter and disillusioned. It happened on a bright, autumn Chicago day.

It was sweater weather, gray and the sun peeking through now and then and the wind toward the lake. The football season was to start that Saturday. The big red streetcar moved down Sixty-third Street under the El tracks like a big bug in a tunnel. It was crowded by the time it reached South Park Avenue. A nice crowd. A laughing, friendly, teasing brown and black crowd. When it reached Stewart and the crowd tumbled off, laughing and loud, there was another car on the corner across the street, an eastbound streetcar, and its crowd was mixed: black, brown and white.

The sun was out now and the students would be sitting on the low concrete wall in front of the school, some on the porch of the sweets shop across the street, the girls laughing soft and low, their teeth flashing white in their brown faces. The leaves should be dropping off the trees and a football silhouetted against the blue, gray and white sky, a black-jack game in the alley and the school cop ready to saunter conspicuously across the street a few minutes before the bell rang, to see that the gamblers weren't late.

It wasn't like that. It was frozen. The few smiles were frozen, the sullen looks and the uncertain frowns were frozen, the battered football lay on the sidewalk unnoticed and the laughter deep down in a pretty brown breast was frozen and the group of white faces on the steps of the frame house across the street from the school were frozen with bleak, determined looks. Then it started, from the porch, from the white faces, low and weak and then getting stronger—"Old Black Joe."

"I hear those darkies' voices gently calling . . ."

No breathing in brown throats and then a slow movement to the curb and the bored cops in the squad car on the corner didn't look bored anymore. The singing faltered for a second and then the voices got stronger.

"I hear those darkies' voices gently calling . . ."

In the street now and the squad car turning its engine over and no laughter and no smiles and now fear in pretty blue eyes, a defiant sneer above a black leather jacket and a sign pulled into view: WE WON'T GO TO SCHOOL WITH NIGGERS ANYMORE.

"I hear those voices gently calling . . ."

A ring around the porch now, a black and brown ring and the black leather jackets and blue eyes and blue jeans and white faces, black hair and blonde hair, on the porch, standing on the steps now and hate, hate in white faces, in brown faces, in black faces.

A white handkerchief flashed in the sun, was wrapped around black knuckles, and another, the sun glinted on a knife blade and the street was full now and the squad car pulling out from the curb, and the cop talking into the microphone.

"I hear those voices . . ."

White handkerchief around black knuckles and knives along their legs and no more song and no one seemed to breathe. A bottle shattered on a curb and a tense black boy moved toward the porch, the bottle's jagged neck in his fist.

"Look out. Gonna get me a goddamn ofay today."

The cops out of the car, then in the car, the black boy inside and the crowd moving around the car, pressing close and fear now in the fat, flaccid faces inside, not bored anymore. The car rocking, rocking, rocking in a sea of faces, black faces, brown faces, yellow faces. Fear and hate and curses and then a voice. A bass voice from a brown face, over the crowd noises, clear:

"I hear those darkies' voices gently calling . . ."

The crowd picking it up and the car rocking in rhythm.

"Let him out, white man. Let him out or we open this car like a sardine can and come get him. And we get you too, white man, we get you good."

"Get back, go on to school, you kids."

"I hear those voices . . ."

"Let him out."

The car rocking in a dark sea.

"Better let him go, Jim. They got some squads on the way."

The black boy back in the street, the crowd milling around. Then a movement toward the forgotten porch, empty now, the leather jackets, the long hair, the blue eyes and blue jeans gone and the sign on the steps—WE WON'T GO TO SCHOOL WITH NIGGERS ANYMORE.

No song and no smiles, the sun is out and it's sweater weather with the first football game Saturday, but no laughter from pretty brown throats, no blackjack game in the alley, no football against the sky, and the sun on a sign on the porch.

The martini was sour with the memory. He put it down and left the apartment. The stereo would shut itself off automatically. As he closed the door, he heard Broonzy: "If you white, all right. If you brown, stick around; but if you're black, get back, get back . . ."

He walked out into the warm air of the street and began walking, ignoring the car. He found himself on East Forty-seventh at Drexel Boulevard. He crossed, and answering the smell of broiling barbecue, he walked into a shop on the north side of the street and ordered a plate of short ribs with medium-hot sauce. He walked outside and headed west again, took the paper plate from the bag and holding it in his left hand, tore off a rib, eating as he walked. Except for the passing motorized National Guard patrols, the ghetto seemed normal again. The burning had been light this far east; west of South Park Boulevard it was much worse. He finished the ribs, coleslaw and French fries just the other side of Langley, wiped his hands on the paper napkin, then rolled the bones in the paper plate and bag; placed it in a garbage can.

He stopped in front of a record store and entered; there was an Otis Redding record playing on the speaker outside. The girl behind the counter was dancing to the music and Freeman joined her; they smiled at one another across the counter. He pointed to the 45 rpm record on the turntable when it had finished and the girl placed it in a bag for him.

"Sweet thing, what time you get off work?" he said.

"Sorry, baby, but my old man's picking me up, you know, Uncle Tom?"

"Well, I sure wouldn't want to mess with him; but every chick I see says that's her old man." He smiled.

"Well, baby, he could be any of 'em. He could even be my old man."

"Sure could, so treat him right."

"Honey, I been taking good care of him since the thing started. He was out in them streets night it started and he wasn't nothing but man."

"Whole lot of men got made that night."

"Better believe it; lots of cats walkin' tall out there and chicks diggin' it."

And she was right. There was pride and defiance in the ghetto in place of sullenness and despair. There were jokes about the National Guard everywhere. Freeman stood on a street corner and watched four men "loud-talking" for a small audience of their friends. Each would sustain a comic monologue as long as he could about the white soldiers of the National Guard and would have to move offstage for another when his comic inventiveness became exhausted. Freeman moved on, still chuckling. Thirsty, he turned into a small dark bar.

He paused just inside the door, allowing his eyes to accustom themselves to the gloom. Recognizing a woman at the bar, he walked over to her.

"Hello, Mrs. Duncan. Mind if I join you?"

"Fine."

He motioned to the bartender and ordered a Ballantine's ale. "How's your son? He hasn't been hanging out on the block and some of the boys are worried about him."

"Shorty don't have time to hang out; he got a job now, making good money. Just bought me a new color TV."

"The boys say he's not just pushing, but he's hooked."

"Now, he ain't really no junkie. I mean, sure he shoot up every now and then, but most of the kids do that nowadays; they don't seem to like whiskey much. He say he ain't hooked. I don't imagine he got more than a twenty-, thirty-dollar-a-week habit and that ain't no habit at all. Woman down the hall where I live, now she got a habit. If she don't get a fix when she need it, well, we all got to go down there and hold her down and clean up when she get sick and all. Sometime us people got to be with her day and night; we got to take turns. Now that's a habit. My son ain't got nothing like that, no sir!"

"Did you ever think he might wind up in jail?"

"Not 'less somebody put some heat on the precinct station and the fuzz need to bust somebody and then he won't have to do more'n five, six months and the people he work for be putting money away for him all that time. But they like him a lot, say he a smart boy, so I don't think they choose him to get busted, even if the heat's on."

"Does he ever think about going back to school?"

"He don't want no part of school. You know how them teachers is, they hate us and sometimes the colored ones the worst. How come they hate us?"

"Fear."

"What they got to be afraid of? Seem like they got everything going for them."

"Did you ever think Shorty might get some kind of regular employment?"

"Mr. Freeman, don't start comin' on like a social worker. Everybody know you hip to our scene. You about the only social worker they got any time for. How he going to get a job? Time was, when I first come up from down South, there was plenty work, but there ain't nothing nowadays. Steel mills done automated and the stockyards moved to them states where they don't like unions."

"You mean the states with the right-to-work laws?"

"Yeah, them states don't like unions. And the factories moving, too.

And down South! Ain't that something? We come up here to work in 'em and they move the factories back where we come from. Mr. Freeman, you know it ain't no work for us, 'less it's out there in them streets."

"Yeah," he said softly, almost to himself. He finished his beer, motioned the bartender and paid for hers as well. "Well, tell Shorty I said hello."

"I sure will. He just like the rest of the boys; think you really swinging. Thanks for the drink." She returned her attention to television as he left the bar. He ran into Shorty, dapper in a lightweight suit, skinny-brim straw hat and wrap-around shades.

"Hey, Turk, how you doin'?"

"Cool, Shorty. Just saw your mother inside."

"She been kinda worried about what's been happenin'. Think we can do anything to help her?"

Freeman turned to look at the bar. "No, Shorty," he said as he moved away, "she doesn't need any help from us."

He slowly retraced his steps along Forty-seventh, walking home. It was dusk now, a few hours before curfew. The streets were full of people, the neon flashing, red, pink and blue on the dark skins of their faces. He listened to the music and sounds of his home, sniffed the smells. He turned south on Drexel Boulevard and walked along the almost deserted street toward Drexel Square. Automobiles made a wide circuit of the riot area in case there might be another outbreak. The hot air became hotter and more still, there was no breeze blowing at all; then there was a faint stirring from the lake to the east and the first faint smell of rain. He had just crossed Fiftieth Street when the first big drops came down splashing on the pavement still hot from the day's sun. The rain increased and there was first the musty smell of the concrete sidewalks, then the sharper smell of the asphalt and as it increased, the clean green smell of the trees and grass.

One thing about Chicago, he thought; even in the ghetto there are trees and grass. He smiled to himself. That's supposed to make being black and poor all right. When Watts happened, all them white folks saying, "What they rioting for? Why, they got palm trees in that slum!" A palm-tree-lined slum; it could only happen in America. It was raining harder now and Freeman walked easily through the now deserted street, the cool rain feeling good on his skin. Suddenly, he began to run, slowly at first and then, as his muscles became warm and loose, faster.

It was dark now, the streets beautiful in the faint light from the street lamps and apartment windows, the trees and grass a translucent green. He ran across the street onto the broad strip of grass which ran down Drexel. *If a cop comes along now I'm a dead nigger. Any nigger running at night has got to have done something wrong.* He smiled to himself and sprinted the last hundred yards to Drexel Square. He stood near the fountain listening to the water running in it, to the sound of the rain on the streets and pavement. The rain had awakened the clean smell of Washington Park just across Cottage Grove and from somewhere in the large kitchenette apartment building behind him he could hear someone playing James Brown.

He walked to Fifty-fifth Street and then east to his apartment building. It was still raining when he entered his apartment, his clothing soaked. He undressed in the bathroom and took a very hot shower, then went into the kitchen, wearing his terry-cloth robe. Even after the barbecue he was hungry and he prepared a cheese omelet and washed it down with Carlsberg beer. He walked into the living room and looked at the unfinished martini he had abandoned when the apartment and his cover, the things he was doing, had closed in on him. He took the glass into the kitchen, poured out the warm martini and rinsed the glass.

He thought of Shorty's mother as he mixed himself a scotch highball, walked into the living room and put Muddy Waters on the turntable. He sat listening to his Mississippi delta sound: "I'm ready, ready's anybody can be . . ."

# 17

**F**reeman met with his staff, Dean, Scott, Stud and Pretty Willie, one night in the back of the poolroom. The riots had continued for four nights and the calling up of the National Guard seemed imminent, but the mayor was milking the riots for every bit of sympathy and publicity that he could muster; his picture was in every paper, there were shots of him on the television newscasts blaming the rioting on Communists and agitators, speaking in his flat, unattractively nasal voice. Politicians were falling over themselves to get into the spotlight and say their piece, having run out of anything new to say about Vietnam. Since the National Guard would be under the control of the governor, the mayor was reluctant to request its use to put down the riots, but there was increasing pressure to call in troops and Freeman figured they would be in within twenty-four to thirty-six hours at the most.

The rioting had leapfrogged from the twenty-four-square-block area originally cordoned off and police chased groups in an area as far north as Roosevelt Road and as far south as Sixty-first, and the Negroes in the West Side ghetto, led by the Comanches, were getting into the act. The police by now were exhausted and resorting to guns more often. The official total of dead was now placed at twenty-eight, none of them white.

"OK, that's the scene. We make our move on Sunday, but since it looks as if the guard will move in tomorrow night or the day after, we'll have to move some of our equipment outside of the ghetto and stash it. If they impose a curfew and set up checkpoints, we'll have to slip out the best way we can.

"Daddy will handle the command post; we'll use Stud and Willie's attack teams, and Willie's will handle the demolition. Stud's team will provide cover. We don't want any shooting if we can help it, we'll have plenty of that later. Right now we want to hit whitey in his own territory and make him look silly. The white man can handle a put-down, but a put-on hangs him up.

"Now, the timing has to be perfect or it spoils the propaganda effect. We want a series of dramatic incidents to advertise our existence, and then we can get down to the dirty work we've been training for. We'll go over this thing in detail, just like with the bank job, every night until H-hour."

When Freeman left through the back entrance of the poolroom, they were huddled over the plans spread on a pool table.

He had been in the streets every night since the riots began. The activity was not as intense, except at sporadic moments when a particular act by the cops would arouse people at a spot here and there in the area. Nevertheless, the people of the neighborhood continued to hit back whenever they could. The women shouted insults at the police, white or black, or ignored them as if they did not exist, even when following their orders. The arrests continued in an effort to break the rioting by jailing the "ringleaders and troublemakers." The police spent a great deal of time looking for Black Nationalists and Communists, but the riots had been going on for three days before they could produce a leaflet having any Marxist-Leninist overtones. The ambulances and vans, full of the arrested, moved regularly in and out of the area.

Emergency rations had to be brought in because each of the supermarkets had been stripped and many of them gutted by fire. The establishment began to retaliate. Social workers increased their harassment, but the white social workers had to be escorted by police, those few willing to venture into the riot area. Welfare checks were held up; the unemployment compensation office on Forty-seventh and South Park was closed for "renovations"; adult literacy classes were discontinued; playgrounds were closed; the swimming pools in Washington Park were emptied; a curfew of ten o'clock was imposed. Bars, liquor stores and poolrooms were closed. People were stopped in the streets repeatedly by police and searched.

Freeman was known throughout the area by now, by both the police and people. He chatted with the street gangs, not preaching to them, asking few questions, listening when they wanted to volunteer anything and they knew he would not carry tales concerning their raiding and looting to the police. Rioting had been largely reduced to the gangs and the older, more bitter and desperate men, unemployed and without hope. But the rest of the community did not object to their activity; they felt it was past time to let the white man know they existed. Freeman knew they no longer gave a damn. Advocates of nonviolence were trucked in by the police from their normal "integrated" haunts to try and pacify the crowds and were met with general abuse and ridicule.

Each night they met in the closed poolroom and went over their plans for Sunday night. Two days after the first meeting, the National Guard moved into the area. The people were not impressed with them any more than with the police, but they had more weapons and armor. The commander of the guard unit held a press conference full of tough-guy clichés and indicated that he expected a return to law and order immediately, or else. He did not indicate what "or else" meant, but he was used to giving orders and having them obeyed. He did not expect to have any trouble with the inhabitants of the ghetto and was somewhat dismayed that the police had not been able to handle the riots, but he had become convinced that the police mollycoddled hoodlums. He thought that he and his men could show them how it was done.

No one was willing to believe that the rioting was a spontaneous uprising by people disgusted with their lot, least of all the mayor and the politicians. They continued to search frantically for Muslims, Communists, Black Nationalists and agitators of any political kind, stripe or spectrum and proudly displayed any they could arrest for incitement to riot or any literature, pamphlet or signs they could uncover. The mayor had often blamed Republicans for his trouble, but felt that Communists and agitators were more appropriate scapegoats for the rioting. A drab, colorless figure, he was known nationally as a powerful politician in his party, but he was almost a nonentity outside of Chicago. Now his picture was in papers everywhere and he began to think in terms of national office for the first time in his career.

The National Guard commander, Colonel Archie "Bull" Evans, shared a common trait among military officers—he was a loud-mouth fool. He had tried to stay in the regular army after the war, but could not bear giving up his gold major's leaves for the stripes of a staff sergeant and returned to his hardware store in suburban Aurora, joining the National Guard and in the ensuing years attaining the rank of full colonel, commanding an infantry National Guard regiment.

His regiment was sloppily trained and ill-disciplined but because of the colonel's mania concerning spit and polish, impressive in garrison and on the parade grounds. The colonel himself was a model of military dandyism, as impressive in uniform as he was nondescript in mufti. He wore a beret of infantry blue and the infantry-blue ascot, preknotted and with hidden snaps, at his throat. There were the green tabs of the combat officer on his epaulets, pinned there by the regimental insignia, his uniforms were tailor-made and of tropical worsted or tropical gabardine. He wore spit-shined paratrooper boots made for him by a bootmaker in London. He wore a pearl-handled, silver-plated Colt .38 and carried a malacca swagger stick. The colonel wore his hair in a close-cropped military brush and surrounded himself with short staff officers to minimize the effect of his five-foot-seven-and-a-half-inch height. He had a short, thick neck and powerful shoulders and arms and a deep chest and he loved to arm-wrestle larger men and beat them.

Colonel Evans's first press conference was a near disaster and the television crew was relieved that they were filming on tape instead of live because of his profanity. He told the members of the press that he intended teaching the people of the area respect for law and order and that there would be no further nursemaiding of them. He said that he did not believe in special treatment for Negroes. They should stop whining and start working and earn the respect of the white citizenry by demonstrating their worth. Within twenty-four hours he announced that things were back to normal and that "they are back on the bottom and we are back on top."

"Man," said Freeman after reading Evans's comments in the papers and observing him on television, "that cat couldn't be any better for us if we ordered him special."

Within thirty-six hours Evans had solidly united the inhabitants of the riot area, many of whom had tired of the rioting and disruption, a public-relations feat of major proportions. Freeman observed the guard unit with an ex-infantry company commander's trained eye and noticed its defects beneath the glitter.

"It's a jive outfit, not much better trained than a boy-scout troop. They're a drag by National Guard standards. First sign of pressure, though, and they're going to be trigger-happy as hell. They'll probably waste a lot of people.

"But when we're ready, they won't be hard to get rid of at all. Man, that colonel is so stupid, I wonder how come he's not a general."

They had checked weapons and explosives in three large suitcases in the checkroom at Union Station. Three went to the checkroom wearing the red caps of the station's porters and checked out the suitcases. Freeman watched it all through the plate-glass window of the coffee shop across the big station floor. They got the suitcases with no trouble, passed the coffee shop without looking at Freeman and went up the stairs to the street above. It was a short distance from the train station to City Hall, their destination. There was a bit more than an hour, so Freeman ordered breakfast, eating it slowly and reading about the riots and Vietnam in a newspaper propped against a sugar bowl. He left when he had eaten and walked to an empty corner of the station, sat on a bench and pretended to be asleep. He had purchased a ticket on the train leaving for Memphis, in case a cop might think him a vagrant or bum catching some sleep in the cool station.

At a few minutes to three he entered one of the empty phone booths and dialed the number of the Chicago *Sun-Times*. He asked for Victor Feldman.

"Mr. Feldman, I have a beat for you. I understand you like that kind of thing. That is the right word, beat? They stopped using scoop in the movies in the thirties, I understand."

"Who is this?"

"Uncle Tom, the official spokesman for the Black Freedom Fighters of America. We are the Chicago chapter of the Mau Mau."

"Look, buddy, if this is some kind of gag, I'm not in the least bit amused."

"No gag, baby, and if your watch has a sweep second hand, you can time it. In exactly forty-eight seconds you will hear an explosion. Down there on the river, you should be able to hear it very well. Thirty-six seconds, now.

"The explosion will be that of the mayor's nice new office in the nice new city hall, which was built by very, very few black men because of those nasty building-trade unions, you know. When the smoke clears, the office will be something of a mess.

"I think you ought to be able to hear something now." Freeman could hear nothing inside the big railroad station, but he heard a muffled roar through the telephone receiver at his ear. "That's it, Mr. Feldman. Now, you can discount any speculation by the mayor or police that this was an assassination attempt that failed. We blew it when we wanted and as an advertisement that we mean business.

"We want the National Guard out of the ghetto, or we will run them out. Then we can talk about how to improve things for the people there, dig? I'll keep in touch, Mr. Feldman. It's not that we trust you, dig, but you like having a beat and you might print the truth, if it's exclusive. There hasn't been much truth printed about what's been happening on the South Side, lately. Remember, we blew the mayor's office when we wanted, when it was empty and he was home in bed. Nobody would want to make that ass into a martyr. Bye now." He hung up, went outside and drove home. By four o'clock he was asleep.

The blowing of the mayor's office made the front pages of the papers the next morning, but only Feldman's column held anything concerning the phone call and it was played with humor, as if a crank call. It did not surprise Freeman, since the mayor, politicians, newspapers and whites in general would prefer to think it a Communist assassination attempt on the mayor. That was all right with Freeman, because the longer they looked for Communists, the longer they would be looking for whites. The United States Communist Party used Negroes as showpieces and flunkies just like all other American institutions. The best cover they had was the white man's stereotypes concerning Negroes.

He called Feldman the next evening and chided him for not printing his phone call on the front page. He announced that the motorcar of one of the Negro aldermen would be painted yellow and white. "Yellow because he's got no balls and white because that's his favorite color. It's to let him know what his constituents think of him. Good night, Mr. Feldman."

Feldman called the alderman's home, apologized for awakening him and asked if his car was missing. Upon checking, the alderman found that the car was indeed missing and called the police. The police found it parked in a zone reserved for police vehicles just down the street from the precinct station in the alderman's neighborhood. It had been painted yellow and white.

This prank received a small story on page four, as well as half of Victor Feldman's column. But the incidents spread throughout all of Chicago's ghettos by the grapevine and they were discussed everywhere. Jokes were told of how spades had air-conditioned the mayor's office by blowing a hole in the wall. The mayor continued his Communist kick and he was echoed by his black puppet alderman.

Other things began to happen, all predicted by "Uncle Tom" in his nightly phone calls to Feldman. Jeeps which were not well guarded ground to a halt on their patrols, their engines ruined by sugar placed in the gas tanks, other jeeps were found with all the tires sliced. Signs were painted late at night saying "Whitey go home"; prowling military patrols found the frequencies of their radios jammed without warning and the jamming device would abruptly go off the air before it could be traced to its source. One such device did not go off the air and, when traced by triangulation, was found in the trunk of the colonel's personal Buick Riviera. The occupation troops gradually became objects of humor and ridicule and their ineptitude, in spite of their spit and polish, became obvious to the mayor, governor and the city police who resented being replaced by what they considered amateur, part-time soldiers.

The morale of the troops, many of whom were losing pay from their jobs in having been called up, declined sharply and the ridicule of the people plus the constant harassment of practical jokes took their toll. Freeman set up another raid on the most prominent of the radio stations beaming their broadcasts to the ghetto audience. Entering the West Side station wearing nylon-stocking masks, they locked up a Negro disk jockey and two engineers in a storeroom and went on the air.

"Hey, hey, ol' bean and you, too, baby, this is Uncle Tom of the Freedom Fighters, interrupting your favorite program to bring you news of the urban underground dedicated to the cause that Mr. Charlie is a drag and to the inhabitants of occupied territory on the South Side.

"I'd dedicate this program to the happy members of the National

Guard army of occupation as well, but I'm afraid we are fresh out of hillbilly music, the Rolling Stones and the Beatles, even if they are more popular than Christ.

"How are the happy National Guardsmen, soul brothers and sisters? I see all those pictures of those colorless cats playing football with you and handing out CARE packages, or is it just the same old surplus food you been getting, without so much publicity, from the welfare? Anyway, if you believe the newspapers, those are the sweetest white soldiers going—even better than the ones who hand out candy in Vietnam to the kids in the village they just burned. Like, if you believe our free press, they must be the most beloved army of occupation since the dawn of history.

"But we know better, don't we, baby? We know about that fourteen-year-old kid who was shot last week because he didn't move quick enough; about how law and order is being brought to the 'lawless' South Side, but the numbers and dope peddling still swings; about how they spend more time looking for nonexistent Communists than they do polishing brass—and you know, baby, they are the brassest polishing army unit in the world.

"The news is the troops have to go—immediately, if not sooner, and if they don't we will kick them out, including Bull-Head Evans. Now, won't we, baby?

"The Freedom Fighters, the Urban Underground of Black Chicago, now deliver this ultimatum: Get out by Sunday or be prepared for war!

"And now, soul brothers and sisters, before the next message from your sponsors, a few jams—some James Brown, Esther Philips and the sweet, swinging Supremes. Whitey, please go home. We don't want you living next door, either."

When the police arrived, they found the three locked in the storeroom, the propaganda being aired by tape and no one anywhere around. The black Freedom Fighters became the talk of the occupied riot area. Hand-bills appeared announcing their feats until now, including the capture of the radio station, the broadcast and the blowing up of the mayor's office. The bills promised more to come. Colonel Evans ordered the arrest of anyone found with a propaganda handbill in his or her possession and his troops to police the area and pick up the rest of the propaganda leaflets from the streets and alleys.

The radio station was guarded thereafter, but the propaganda broadcasts continued with the disk-jockey format. The first was broadcast from the alleyway not far from the El station on Fifty-first Street. Guardsmen found a Japanese portable tape recorder playing through a loudspeaker attached high in the steel supports of the El tracks. The first guardsman to climb and attempt to tear down the equipment found that it had been booby-trapped with a wire attached to the metal outdoor speaker which led to the third rail. The electric shock hurled him to the ground and he was hospitalized. The broadcast continued for a growing crowd until an electrician disconnected it. Each night at the same time another broadcast would be made from a similar booby-trapped setup; from the roof of an apartment building, a garbage can in an alley, hidden in a newsstand and once through the speakers of an army truck which patrolled the neighborhood announcing orders and dispensing National Guard propaganda which had been stolen and parked in an alley.

The guard was continuously harassed and neither arrest, investigation nor threats could suppress the growing opposition to the troops by both the underground of Freeman's and the populace at large. Evans was furious at being made look a fool by people he held in contempt. He blamed it all on the Communists. "You know they would have neither the guts nor the intelligence for this kind of thing if it were not Communist-inspired, led and directed. Let the Commies get away with this and the entire nation is endangered. We must make our stand here so that the forces of godless communism are not misled concerning our determination to oppose their plans to take over the free world."

The colonel was beginning to embarrass a great many people with his statements, even in a city like Chicago, and his public information officer was used increasingly by the press to water down statements. But he had also become a white hope. Colonel Evans had contempt for the repeated demands by the Freedom Fighters that he and his National Guard be removed or suffer the consequences, and waited with some impatience on the Sunday night of the deadline announced in the communications center of his command post. A bit after two in the morning he retired to view a John Wayne movie on late-night television. The colonel liked John Wayne movies very much. His National Guard unit had taken over the Washington

Park recreation center for their headquarters and command post. The old field house sits facing north and across from the large field containing baseball and softball diamonds, a cricket pitch used by the Negro West Indians of the ghetto and football fields. Separating the field house and the athletic fields is a large drive that cuts through the park from Fifty-fifth Street at Cottage Grove Avenue, ending at South Park Boulevard. The field house sits in front of the swimming-pool complex, built by the WPA during the depression, with two Olympic-size pools and a diving pool. Spectator stands flank the pool to the west, the east is flanked by an eight-foot iron fence and high foliage and to the south is a children's playground. The pool had been refilled for the recreation of the National Guard troops but, since drawing sniper fire, was not used at night. Freeman's reconnaissance revealed that the approach to the field house through the pool area was not guarded.

At 0015, after curfew, Freeman led two attack teams of five men each into Washington Park. A stolen army ambulance stood at the curb facing north on South Park Boulevard, just adjacent to the children's playground which was south of the swimming-pool area. They entered through the playground, scaled the fence, and crossing the unlit and unguarded concrete area which held the two swimming pools and the diving pool, then entered the locker room of the field house, now the command post and personal quarters of the commander of the guard unit on ghetto occupation duty, Colonel "Bull" Evans. The locker room had been converted into a private office and bedroom for the colonel, with the small gymnasium above it used for the communications center for the outfit. Freeman slipped into the colonel's empty office, seated himself behind the colonel's desk, poured a generous shot of Jack Daniel's black label from the bottle on the colonel's desk and watched an old John Wayne western on the television in the corner while awaiting the colonel's return from the communications center. Freeman figured that there must be important messages for the colonel to answer to make him miss the beginning of a western. He thought that the messages might have something to do with Uncle Tom and the Black Freedom Fighters of Chicago.

Upon entering the room, his eyes not yet accustomed to the dim light within, the colonel failed to notice the figure behind the desk until he was only a short distance away, his eyes on Wayne on television whipping three men in a barroom brawl. He was reaching for the bottle of bourbon when he noticed the long-barreled Colt target pistol, a silencer fitted to its barrel, pointed at him by Freeman, a black man, clad in all-black and seated in his chair, behind his desk, a glass of his whiskey at the nigger's elbow. The colonel, ignoring the threat of the silenced pistol, reached, with the foolish instincts of John Wayne, for his holstered, pearl-handled revolver, filling his lungs for a bellow of outrage, cut short by an accurate judo chop behind his left ear by Stud Davis, who caught his limp body before he could fall.

They carried the colonel back the way they had come, and as silently; slim black figures moving swiftly and efficiently through the sultry, moonless Chicago night. They flung the colonel, inside a large mail sack, over the fence like a sack of grain and then into the waiting ambulance, Pretty Willie seated as the driver.

The colonel awakened tied securely to a kitchen chair, his face made up in Jolson blackface with large red lips painted in. The colonel stared back into the dark, silent faces with a look of grim, haughty disdain that would have done justice to Wayne futilely captured by redskins. He watched one of his captors as he carefully placed a drop of liquid onto a sugar cube, and put it into a cup of coffee, then approached the colonel with the cup.

"What was that you put on the sugar?"

"Just a little acid, daddy."

"Acid! You're going to kill me."

"Oh, no, daddy," he said, as the colonel was held and he forced the coffee down his throat, "we're going to let you *live!*"

The next evening, at the time of his usual call, Uncle Tom informed Feldman where the kidnapped colonel could be found at a particular time and place. The colonel was found alive as promised, seated on the edge of the reflection pool of the Fountain of Time, at the southeast corner of Washington Park. The colonel was dangling his bare feet ecstatically in the pool, a look of beatitude on his face.

Upon being medically examined, the colonel was found to be under the influence of LSD and said repeatedly that he had met the "most wonderful niggers in the world."

# 18

The National Guard unit reacted with predictable ferocity to the humiliation of their commander. Never a well-disciplined unit, they now roamed the streets with their weapons fully loaded, a round in the chamber and safeties off, eager for their first kill. The ghetto, with a survival instinct centuries old, faded into their homes and the guard turned their fury on the very streets where a black mob had roamed only a short time before. All undamaged stores were used for target practice, a handful bombed with grenades, under the assumption that they were colored owned. "We're evenin' things up," said one sergeant. Trigger-happy, panicky, smelling the hatred and contempt the ghetto Negroes felt for them, they fired at almost anything that moved and black casualties mounted.

At nightfall, the ghetto hit back and snipers roamed their turf in search of white targets. Poorly armed with pistols, shotguns, surplus WW II M-1 carbines, they proved a poor match for even the ill-trained guard unit, but their effect on the morale of the guard was staggering. Panic increased and the guard's casualties came mainly from their shooting one another accidentally or in fright. A sniper was rumored to be on the roof or in one of the apartments of a three-story building and a half-track with four .50 caliber machine guns mounted was rolled to within fifty yards of the building and the big guns turned on it, pinning the occupants to the glass-strewn floors of their apartments for more than half an hour, killing one mother of four and wounding two others.

Freeman risked roaming the streets, gathering intelligence, noting the command posts, the disposition of the units, the state of their morale, their dwindling discipline.

"Turk, when do we go into action?" asked Stud Davis. They were gathered in the poolroom late that night, Davis, Dean, Scott and Du Bois.

"Tonight. First the sniper teams to keep them panicky, then we hit hard in a few days with our attack teams." They leaned toward him in eager anticipation, ready after the long months of training, for their baptism of fire.

"I want all sniper teams in the field except the reserve. Sugar, you know their sectors of operation, so get the word out. I want the reserve in the field the following night, then operate from that point on with one-third of the teams at a time—so everyone has two nights of rest in between. Daddy, you work out the rotation; Sugar, you figure out logistics and supply; Willie, get to work on propaganda leaflets to be distributed the day following our first hit."

"Turk?" interjected Stud.

"Yeah, Stud?"

"Is it all right if I work solo? I don't mind leading an attack team, but for sniper work I'd rather work alone."

Freeman thought for a minute, then said:

"Tell you what, we'll work together the first night; I'll act as your cover, you command. If I dig your action, OK, but either way, the decision is final."

"OK with me, Turk."

"Right. Willie, you take command of Stud's team. Will that give you time for the leaflets?"

"Yeah, Turk. I'll set things up and the cell can handle it from there. They're damn good; in fact, they could function without me."

"That's the scene we want; nobody indispensable. Now, listen carefully and take notes. Daddy, call the weather station and get the exact time of sundown and sunrise for tomorrow night. I want everyone in a darkened room one hour prior to sundown to start on their night vision and all teams out of the field no later than one hour prior to sunrise. I also want wind direction, wind velocity, temperature and relative humidity transmitted to the teams for calculation for firing.

"A large breakfast is OK, but a light lunch and no liquids or stimulants of any kind after lunch. No more than one cigarette an hour until H-hour. One joint prior to an afternoon nap is all right. We all know the drill. Any questions?"

There were none.

"All right, synchronize watches by radio or telephone tomorrow night at curfew, 2200. H-hour is one hour later, 2300. Move out!"

Stud Davis awakened the next morning precisely at seven, the hour he had decided to awaken the night before, without the aid of an alarm. He was alert the moment he opened his eyes. He lived in a single-room kitchenette with small bathroom and shower. It was in the rear of a large kitchenette apartment building and included a back porch overlooking the El tracks. The room was neat and spare; it had a combination gas range and refrigerator, a television set tucked into one corner, two chairs, a card table covered with oilcloth and a transistor radio seated on a small table near the head of the bed which doubled as a couch.

Stud arose, walked into the bathroom, rubbed his light beard and decided he did not need a shave. After washing, he returned to the room and slipped into a pair of tight-fitting jeans which he wore only at home. He put on a percolator, and while awaiting the coffee, ate a large bowl of cornflakes with sliced bananas while listening to his favorite radio station. He drank the coffee, then ate four fried eggs and bacon, washing it down with half a quart of milk. Not until then did he have his first cigarette of the day. He snubbed out the butt, washed the dishes and tidied the room, a spotless oasis in the smelly, dirty building. He had a thing about cleanliness.

He left his apartment and walked the few blocks to the poolroom for the final briefing before the night's action. He moved loose and easy, fighting the heavy drowsy feeling he had always felt before an important athletic contest because it was much too early; that afternoon was soon enough and he would allow it to grow gradually until the release of the first round fired. It had been much the same in each of the sports in which he had excelled; you controlled the feeling and used it, not the other way around.

He sat silent through the final briefing, offering no contribution and asking no questions. Freeman asked him to stay after the others had left.

"I'll be your cover, Stud, but the scene is yours tonight. As I said in the briefing just now, we'll be operating as a roving team in sector six. Our first target will be the quad fifty; after that targets of opportunity."

Stud smiled tightly.

"I saw what that thing did to the building; I never thought a machine gun could do that much damage to bricks and concrete."

"It's a bitch of a weapon and multiplied by four you got something else. One of the little girls who was in that building screams constantly every time they take her off tranquilizers. I want that gunner."

"I saw him on TV; he looked like he was sorry the building was still standing," said Stud.

Freeman pointed to a map of the area.

"They're usually stationed here. We'll approach this way and fire from the roof of this building; that way they'll have to swing the gun mount a full 180 degrees to bring them to bear on our position after they spot us and by that time we should have got in our shots and been long gone.

"We both go after the gunner and after he's hit, you take targets from twelve to six o'clock and I take them from six to twelve. Don't get greedy and don't wait for them to locate us; when we get in our rounds, we move on. OK?"

Stud nodded.

"I don't doubt you can work solo, but I have to check you out this way so the cats don't think you get special treatment." Stud smiled broadly. "I'll see you at the rendezvous tonight. Easy, Stud."

Stud picked up his dismantled weapon and ammunition, one of the .03 sniper rifles with scope. He returned to his apartment, cleaned and oiled it, checked its moving parts and the scope, then wrapped it in a lightly oiled cloth and placed it beneath his bed. He washed away all traces of oil from his hands, carefully cleaning his nails as he did so. He turned on his small television set, found nothing to his liking, then lay on the couch listening to the radio until time to fix lunch.

Burkhardt had risen to Freeman's bait and after working on a .22 rifle range several evenings with the gang leaders, all on their best behavior, "sir"-ing him until dizzy, he agreed to coach a larger group. It was Stud who sold him, and Burkhardt was enthusiastic about his potential as a marksman.

"This boy Davis," he said to Freeman, "is the best natural rifleman I've ever seen. You're sure he's had no previous experience with a rifle?"

"I'm certain, Mr. Burkhardt," Freeman replied.

"Amazing!" said Burkhardt, watching Stud firing prone on the University .22 range. "Why, he's potential Olympic team caliber. I'm certain he'll be able to do well in the National Junior Championships in less than a year."

"If he sticks with it," said Freeman. "He loses interest in anything as soon as he's mastered it. As soon as he really becomes good with a rifle, he probably won't even want to see one."

But Freeman was wrong. Stud Davis had finally found his métier, the one thing which quieted the fear he hid so well. He never saw a bull at the center of the target, but always a man, any man. In less than two months he was a better marksman with a rifle than Freeman.

To Burkhardt's chagrin, but not Freeman's surprise, the National Rifle Association refused their application for membership and the club broke up; but ten of the Cobras had had several months of intensive training on a rifle range.

Scott and Dean left the poolroom together. "You goin' home now, Daddy?"

"Naw. I better check with all the leaders of the sniper teams, make sure everything groovy."

"Turk said to cool it until tonight."

"It's all right; Turk will understand. Cool it."

Scott walked home and spent the afternoon figuring the formulas for the flight trajectory of a .30 caliber bullet for various angles and ranges. Mathematics always relaxed him.

Freeman spent the morning at the office, left just before lunch, announcing he would tour the riot area and made a last-minute check of the positions to be attacked. They had not been moved.

He returned to his apartment, cooked and ate a light lunch, went to his bedroom and slept until late evening. He awakened to the first sound of the alarm and dressed in the dark. He met Stud at the appointed rendezvous, both dressed in dark clothing, including low-cut black sneakers, wearing wraparound sunglasses to protect their night vision. The other snipers moved in teams of three, one as decoy, the other two as fire team. The decoy was to shoot from opposite the fire team to draw fire, then disappear. The remaining two would then open fire from behind to catch the guardsmen exposed and firing in the opposite direction.

Without a word, Stud and Freeman moved silently over the rooftops and took their position above and beyond the quad fifties mounted on a half track, a WW II vehicle, as was most of the guard's equipment, but deadly nevertheless.

Stud held up two fingers to indicate a range of two hundred yards. Freeman nodded his confirmation. Stud nodded again and they each slipped their arms through the slings, using the roof parapet as a support, jacked a round into the chamber and slipped off the safety. The gunner was seated on the mount smoking a cigarette and talking to one of the crew. Freeman placed the crosshairs of the scope on his middle and at the sound of Stud's shot, squeezed off his own. Both rounds hit and the gunner dropped to the street, dead before he hit. Stud shot him again as he lay in the street. They both emptied their clips at the scattering crew below, reloaded and disappeared as silently and swiftly as they had come. Across the rooftops came the scattered firing of other teams in action. The war had begun.

That night the Freedom Fighters killed six, wounded nineteen and received no casualties. Escalation by both sides could be expected. After five nights of sniper activity, Freeman ordered a two-day rest and then ordered his attack teams into the field.

"Same scene as with the snipers; all teams into the field the first night, then a one-third rotation after that. We don't need any heroes; hit and run, hit them when they least expect it, then disappear as soon as they deploy and return your fire. If they follow too aggressively, ambush them; otherwise, vanish."

Stud Davis moved his attack team down the alley through the moonless night. He could hear the big rats scurry into hiding as they approached and return to their feeding as they passed. He had hunted the rats at night in these same alleys, two boys leading, one with an air rifle, the other with a flashlight. One would fix the rat with the beam of the light and the other would fire. Unless hit exactly right, the BB would stun, but not kill and the other boys would finish the rat with sticks. It was good sport and he had learned that the rats did not fear man, they just got out of your way because it was easier. The rats would often charge the group when cornered if the boy with the air rifle missed.

He was leading the maneuver squad of his team, the fire squad approaching the street which intersected the alley from the opposite block. He halted his men with a hand signal and looked out into the deserted street. It was several hours after curfew and the streets were silent and empty. He checked his watch, then motioned his men into cover at the alley mouthway and behind parked cars a short distance away. He saw that across the street the fire squad was already in place. His maneuver squad of five were each armed with a hunting knife, pistol, grenades, three with shotguns, the other two with semiautomatic carbines. The fire team were all equipped with weapons on full automatic.

He heard the patrol approach, two jeeps much too close together, containing four men each; the driver, a rifleman and two tending the mounted machine gun at the rear of the vehicle. Stud waited until they were about ten yards away, stood and threw a grenade. Four others followed suit and they all ducked for cover. The explosions followed quickly upon one another and the sharp staccato of automatic fire echoed the loud thumps of the grenades. One jeep lay on its side, the other had crashed a parked car. Stud signaled and the fire ceased. He led his maneuver team cautiously toward the ambushed patrol, their guns at the ready. He turned off the ignition of each jeep in turn and motioned his men to strip the bodies of guns and ammunition.

One boy of about nineteen, Stud's age, moved feebly in a pool of his own blood, shock and surprise on his face. Stud paused to look at his face. He might have played basketball against him. He bent to take his weapon and ammunition.

The boy asked, over and over: "Why? Why? Why?"

Stud bent close, so that the boy could hear, and said: "Because it's war, whitey."

They finished and in seconds the dark of the alley swallowed them up. The rats moved from their burrows sniffing the strange smells in the air, the bolder and more curious ones moving toward the compelling smell of blood. The rest returned to their feeding and the occupied ghetto was silent once again.

# 19

Colonel Evans had been relieved of his command after his kidnapping, although the newspapers indicated he was recovering from injuries received during his heroic escape from his hoodlum captors. The president, acting on requests from the governor of Illinois and the mayor of Chicago, ordered a brigade of the Eighty-second Airborne Division airlifted from Fort Bragg, North Carolina, to Chicago to relieve the National Guard unit.

Brigadier Scott, commander of the airborne brigade, met with Lieutenant Colonel Jensen, acting commander of the National Guard unit of occupation, in the guard's headquarters for a debriefing session.

"Dammit, Colonel," said the brigadier, "you mean military troops can suffer the kind of casualties you've taken from a bunch of unorganized hoodlums?"

"It's far worse than that, sir," replied Jensen. "Someone has trained those bastards and they've been trained well. And they have military weapons, most of them automatic."

"How could they get their hands on weapons of that kind?"

"It must be the gang who robbed the National Guard Armory," said a quietly dressed civilian who had been allowed to attend the debriefing. "There was no publicity because the press agreed to a blackout while we investigated.

"They have a pretty good arsenal: M-14 and -16 rifles and ammo, grenades and launchers, communications equipment, the works. In the crowded slums where they operate and you can't use your heavy weapons, they can match your firepower."

"The sons of bitches!" said the brigadier grimly. "And we thought it would be another operation like Detroit last summer. What kind of tactics are they using, Colonel?"

"Hit-and-run attacks and ambushes; they won't stand and fight. Usually groups of from five to eight operating in tandem, each with a section leader and the entire unit commanded by one man. They demonstrate knowledge of fire and maneuver, small-unit tactics and seem well disciplined."

"The Commies must be at the bottom of this. Where else could they get that kind of training?"

"You're probably right, General Scott," said the civilian. "I'm certain the Russians have smuggled in one or more of their top agitprop agents and I'm requesting counterinsurgency teams from Washington today."

"Agitprop?"

"Agitation and propaganda, experts in the creation of chaos, insurgency and revolution."

"They wouldn't dare," said the colonel.

"That's what we said about the Cuban missiles." The brigadier turned to his adjutant.

"I want the patrols doubled tonight, weapons on full automatic and the orders are to shoot anything moving after curfew. Shoot to kill."


The members of Freeman's recruitment and training cells had been organizing and training units in twelve major cities since the first of the year. Freeman considered nine of the underground units combat ready, the remaining three marginal. He ordered operations in Chicago reduced to harassment and ordered his twelve other units into action. He awaited the effects of his escalation of the war.

They had left during the bitter cold of early January, the quick-witted hustlers of the gang, those most likely to think, adjust, survive on any ghetto street. They were to submerge themselves in new identities, establish a cover and recruit, organize and train those street gangs in their new cities which were most like the Cobras of Chicago.

They left with sealed orders for a temporary destination within a two-hundred-mile radius of Chicago. The orders indicated their new area of operation and contained cash, various documents of identification and the name of a bank where funds could be drawn under their new names.

They moved into the teeming ghettos, their new homes, each a seed of rebellion planted in fertile soil.

Freeman had patiently built up an intelligence network: bus and taxi drivers, the drivers of mail trucks, postmen, delivery and messenger boys, anyone who would be able to circulate freely after the riots had begun; garbage men, street cleaners. He recruited six medical students, two interns and a young surgeon, plus eight trained nurses. He was extremely careful in attempting to recruit anyone from the black middle class, but found to his surprise that a growing number shared the attitudes of their less fortunate black brothers. He felt that if the Ku Klux Klan could infiltrate the Chicago police force, there was no reason the Cobras couldn't as well. In a short time he recruited six uniformed policemen and two detectives. He still hoped to recruit Dawson as his chief double agent and second-in-command.

He knew that inevitably the cumbersome bureaucratic machinery of the nation's law-enforcement agencies would begin their search to destroy him.

The general personally accompanied the CIA counterinsurgency teams to Chicago to supervise the setup of their operation. Shortly after arrival, he met with the hand-picked members of the group, code named: Operation Law and Order.

"It will be SOP for this kind of operation: infiltrate a paid informer; identify and place on our payroll a defector as a double agent; divide, confuse, bore from within. Our primary target is their leader, undoubtedly a Soviet professional. Cut off the head and the snake will die.

"Whoever he is, we should give the man due professional credit for organizing ignorant slum dwellers into a fighting unit as effective as so far proven. Until we crush this insurgency, we operate around the clock."

Three evenings later, Freeman received a phone call at his apartment. It was a vaguely familiar woman's voice who asked if she could come to his apartment within the hour, but refused her name. She said that it was urgent. By now, Freeman was operating under strict security measures. He assumed that all except public phones chosen at random were bugged. He made standard checks for a tail whenever he went to a rendezvous which could not be explained by his normal duties with the foundation. He therefore regarded the mysterious call with suspicion.

He took out a Colt Woodsman .22, checked the mechanism and loaded a clip. He generally mistrusted automatics and never left a clip fully loaded so as not to weaken the spring. He slid the clip into the butt, jacked a round into the chamber, made sure the safety was on, and sat listening to music while he awaited the arrival of his visitor.

A half-hour later, the bell rang and he walked to the door of his apartment, pressed the buzzer to let the visitor in from the outer hall. He checked the door to make sure that no one was already waiting for him and then cracked it enough to see the elevator. He held the gun at his side, the safety on, but ready to fire.

The elevator stopped at his floor and the door opened. She stepped out and looked for the number of his apartment, then approached his door. Freeman slid the Colt behind a bookcase near the door then opened it wide to greet her. He noticed how well the red dress went with the rich black of her skin.

"I'll be damned," he said, "the Dahomey queen." He opened the door wide as he smiled in greeting and stepped back to let her enter. She walked down the short hallway to the living room, turned in the middle of the room to smile at him shyly. She wore her hair natural, kinky, and the same short length all around her head, no straightening irons, no oil. There were large gold hoop earrings that emphasized the beauty of her slim long neck. She wore no lipstick, just a touch of makeup to bring out the almond shape of her eyes.

"Baby, you're beautiful. Sit down and let me fix you a drink. Johnny Walker black label, isn't it? I'll be right back and then you'll have to tell me what you've been doing since the last time I saw you and what you're doing here in Chicago." He returned with the drinks, then moved to the stereo. "Let's see if I can remember the jams you dig.

"So what are you doing here and how did you find me?" Freeman was on guard because he had never told her his name and she had never asked it; they hadn't that kind of arrangement. Then he remembered, she did know his name. They had been stopped in Washington one night by a cop and there had been the usual scene; he had to show Freeman, himself, and far more important, Freeman's woman, that Freeman simply did not count as a man. Freeman had endured it until the policeman threatened to search her and he had intervened, showing him his ID. Until then, she had known him only as Dan and she had wondered aloud why a District of Columbia cop would call any Negro "Mr. Freeman, sir."

"Well, I got to be here in Chicago for a few days and I thought I'd look you up and say hello. There ain't that many Freemans in the book with your first name and I got you the third time around. You know, you used to talk about Chicago all the time. Never could figure out if it drug you or you dug the place; seemed sometime like both scenes.

"I ain't hustlin' no more. Got me a sponsor, turned me on to a down pad out in North East D.C. and he sponsors the whole scene. I even save bread out of what he lays on me and I got a part interest in a bar. When the scene is over, I won't have to hustle no more. Bought a little property, too. Oh, he a good trick, honey, and not too bad for an ofay." She paused and looked directly at him. "You know him. You used to work for him." Freeman sipped his drink and looked at her, saying nothing. "He's out here to step on the Freedom Fighters and the cat started it all."

"Let's dance, baby." He moved to the amplifier and turned the volume up, then brought her to the center of the room, holding her close, his mouth close to her ear. "If the room is bugged they won't pick us up from here, not with the music. All right," he said, "run it on down."

"I figure you might know some of those cats and they'd want to know what's happen' downtown."

He held her a bit more tightly. He wondered if he would have to kill her. Had she guessed anything on her own, or had she been sent to him? "What makes you think I might know any of the FF?"

"OK, maybe you don't, but you could get the word out. You know the city and I don't. You the only one I know here and they need to know."

"Why you sticking your neck out?"

She leaned away from him and gazed at him fiercely. "I'm black, ain't I?" He nodded and pulled her back into his arms.

"Who's this cat I'm supposed to have worked for?"

"The general. You know who he is and you know what he does. He thinks he pretty cool, but he talk more than he think. Course, he don't think I got enough brains to know what's goin' on but a little piece here, little piece there; put it together and you got something." She described the general.

There was no doubt, she knew him. "Met him at this big place some big brass from the Pentagon own over on the tidewater. They had a lot of chicks out, every kind, every color. Them Pentagon cats pretty freakish, everybody in D.C. know that. Great big pad, swimming pool, boat, place to shoot and shotguns and shit everywhere. About a dozen whores and maybe five or six studs. The general was there and we spent all the time together. He dug my action and he got a big thing for dark meat. He a little bit freakish, but nothing really way out.

"He been my sponsor ever since. Almost a year now. Well, baby, he really flippin' out about these Black Freedom Fighters, thinks it a Communist scene. They want to find the ofay behind it and the head nigger and stomp on 'em. Ain't gonna be no arrest and trial if they get 'em . . .

"Yeah, baby, you worked for him. For a long time I didn't think so—he talk 'bout you all the time. You know, you *his* nigger? First time he call you name, I think he talkin' about you, but the cat he talkin' about ain't nothing like I knew you; then it start addin' up, must be the same cat: Chicago, same looks, live in the same place. I looked you up in the phone book after that time the fuzz stop us and you lived out in Anacostia, but I didn't call you. Didn't think you'd dig that, but I just want to know where you live. Anyway, after awhile I knew it the same cat, you, and you got to be puttin' one of us on and it got to be the general. If you come on like a Tom all that time, you got to have a reason. Never know you to do nothin' without you know just what you want and why. So that's how I know how to find you and why I think you can hip the cats the general wants to waste."

He had her describe the setup as best she could. He could fill in the gaps. It was a typical stakeout, a bit more elaborate than most. They had manpower, communications, weapons, and from her description of the few she had seen, some of their top agents. And they would have more money than anyone else in the game. They always had bread and sometimes they got lazy because they had. But they wouldn't be lazy now. Hunting down niggers would be a new scene.

"Who's in charge?"

"I don't know," she said, "he ain't here yet. Coming in from overseas in a couple days. General says he the best agent they got, talk about him a lot. I'll try to find out."

"No, you better not see me again, unless I get to Washington sometime. Maybe one of these days . . ." He looked at her.

"Don't go square on me now. One thing you don't need is a whore. Even a ex-whore."

They continued to dance and he questioned her through Sonny Stitt and half of Ray Charles. Finally he was satisfied and they returned to the couch and he freshened their drinks.

She turned on the couch to look at him. "I don't have to go home tonight."

He reached out slowly and touched her hair. "Baby," he said, "ain't that kinky stuff pretty?"

# 20

O akland blew first, then Los Angeles, then, leapfrogging the continent, Harlem and South Philadelphia. After years of crying conspiracy, the witch hunters found, to their horror, there was a conspiracy afoot among the black masses. Every city with a ghetto wondered if they might be next. The most powerful nation in history stood on the brink of panic and chaos. The Freedom Fighters fought first the police, then the National Guard and finally, the elite troops of the army and marines. Within a week there were major guerrilla uprisings in eight major cities in the United States and efforts to eliminate them had proven futile.

Several days of heavy rain, followed by a cool air mass moving down from Canada, broke the Chicago heat. The city lay under a bright warm sun and at night there was a cool breeze from the lake. The birds began their southern journey and the leaves of the cottonwood, poplar and maple trees began to change color, some of them reluctantly releasing from the limbs to trace a lazy descent to the ground, to be gathered and burned at the curb and produce the pungent smell of autumn come to Chicago. At night the city's silence would be broken by the explosion of grenades, the staccato message of automatic fire. The FF moved easily and silently through the ghetto which offered them affection and support, their coloration finally protective.

The curfew had silenced the streets below and a cleansing breeze from the lake stirred through Freeman's apartment. Miles Davis, mute meeting mike in a sexless kiss, blew bittersweet chocolate tones through the speakers, "My Funny Valentine" becoming a poignant poem of lonely love.

Freeman and Joy sat on the couch, the lights low, the dishes in the sink, an empty wine bottle in the trash, slowly sipping their drinks and

Miles in the room, brooding, black and beautiful, saying his thing on his horn. In the sudden silence as the record changed, Freeman turned to Joy.

"Joy," he asked, "what's bugging you tonight?"

"Those damn Freedom Fighters, as they call themselves. You can't go to a cocktail party nowadays without running into someone who has lost his integrated job.

"My husband," she said with bitterness, "has lost his staff appointment at the hospital, and he was the only Negro doctor in a white hospital in the city."

"What did he have to do with the riots?"

"That's the point: decent, innocent people are suffering. Now they want to get rid of me at the store, I can smell it."

"They can't let you go, baby, you're the best-looking buyer with any department store in the Loop."

"It's nothing to joke about." She took a long swallow of her drink. "People are losing jobs they worked and sacrificed to get, all because of ignorant niggers who know nothing but hate."

Freeman rose to put another record on the changer and John Coltrane's soprano sax gave an oriental flavor to "My Favorite Things."

"Can't you remember, Joy, how it was to live like they do?"

"Don't defend those hoodlums. Those Freedom Fighters," she spat out the words in contempt, "are shooting real guns."

"Didn't figure to take long before some of them realized there's no win in throwing a brick at a man with a gun." Joy took a slow sip of her drink, watching him carefully over the rim of her glass.

"Dan," she asked quietly, "are you mixed up in this?"

"Baby, you got to be kidding," he laughed. "You think I'm stupid enough to get involved in a scene like that? They don't stand a chance."

"You used to talk about this kind of thing when we were in East Lansing. You insisted when everything else failed, Negroes would have to fight."

"Honey," he said reasonably, "I was a kid in college then. And besides, everything else hasn't failed. We're both examples of the kind of progress Negroes have made in the last few years." She searched his face for some clue and he told her what she wanted to hear, calmed her, reassured her.

"Look at all the Negroes we have in influential positions: a member of the presidential cabinet, a Supreme Court justice, a senator. And look at me," he smiled, his arm swept his playboy pad, "I've been poor and, believe me, this is better."

"Honey," she smiled, "I'm being silly. This thing has us all nervous and on edge." She rose gracefully and walked to the door leading to the bedroom. She turned and took off her wig.

"Fix us some more drinks while I get comfortable," and with a smile, she turned and walked into the bedroom. Freeman smiled with some relief. It had been close for awhile, but he was sure he had convinced her. A short time later, lying bathed in sweat, her head on his shoulder, he was certain.


It was hot the next afternoon, but the thick walls of the precinct police station made it cool and comfortable inside and the desk sergeant sat, oblivious to the station smells, working the crossword puzzle in the *Chicago Tribune*. The door opened and a bit of the hot day outside followed a woman who seemed immune to the heat. She walked to the sergeant's desk much like the models he had seen displaying fashions on television and in the newsreels. She wore a small white hat, white gloves and a pale green summer suit of shantung silk. The sergeant could not identify the material, but he knew it was expensive, so he spoke to her with far more respect than was usual for the colored women who normally entered his domain.

"Yes, lady; can I help you?"

"I want to speak with someone," she replied, "about 'Uncle Tom.'"


That evening, Freeman, entering his lobby, found a coded message in his mailbox. It was from one of his double agents on the police force, indicating the police planned a shakedown of the block in which the FF had one of its arms caches. Because there was not much time, he ignored telephone security and, hurrying to his apartment, he phoned from his bedroom, the room lit only by the light in the hallway.

"Daddy? Turk. Listen carefully. The fuzz are shaking down the block where we have a stash, safe house three. Move it right away to safe house six. Cancel tonight's hit if you have to, but get that stuff moved and check back with me." He hung up and light burst into the room from the floor lamp in the corner. In one motion, Freeman whirled, dropped to the floor next to the bed and reached for the pistol he kept beneath the pillow, but the gun was not there.

"Freeze, Freebee," ordered Dawson, "or should I call you 'Uncle Tom.'" He sat in the Saarinen womb chair next to the teak floor lamp, his service Smith & Wesson .38 Police Positive held with easy competence and resting on the right knee of his crossed legs.

"The heat's not under the pillow. I have that one and the rest you had stashed here. You got quite an arsenal for a playboy—that how you get so much trim?"

"Uncle Tom? Not me, baby. You trying to put me on?" and suddenly indignant: "What the hell you doing in my pad pointing a gun at me? I hope you got a search warrant, man."

"Martial law, remember? I don't need a warrant."

"Now you fuzz can continue to do what you always have in the ghetto, only for a change, it's legal. That must take all the kicks out of it." Freeman, his eyes on those of Dawson, began to rise carefully. He had fired on the police range with Dawson; he knew what he could do with that revolver.

"Like I said, Freebee: freeze." Dawson rose from his seat, the gun never wavering. "OK, now stand up very slow and keep your hands where I can see them. Good, now walk over to that wall. Hands as high as you can reach, flat against the wall, you know the drill. Now hold it and don't move." Freeman stood, his weight on his hands flat against the wall and to either side of a Saito woodblock he had purchased in Tokyo. Dawson approached him, deftly searched him, then retreated slowly to the womb chair.

"OK, you can sit on the bed." Freeman walked slowly to the bed and seated himself as close to Dawson as he dared.

"Man, you sure had my nose open, Freebee. Out of all the people in Chicago, I never figured you for Uncle Tom. Cool Dan Freeman, the South Side playboy, nothing on your mind except chicks, clothes, good whiskey and sports cars. A beautiful cover, now I think about it."

"You think I'd risk all this for . . ."

"Save it. I don't know if you are or if you're not Uncle Tom and it's not my job to decide. I have enough evidence to take you in and that's what I'm going to do."

"What evidence?"

"This reel of tape I found here. One of Uncle Tom's propaganda broadcasts you cats run all over the neighborhood from booby-trapped recorders."

"I don't know anything about that."

"You know, right up until I found this I didn't believe it. Didn't even bother to bring my partner along. After I searched the place I was going to wait for you and apologize for having to check out the lead."

"That's mighty white of you."

"Who's the white man running things?"

"How come there's got to be an ofay running things?"

"You know the Communist Party in the States is like any other white scene: a few showpiece spades in the name of integration, but whitey calling the shots."

"And, of course, a spade couldn't possibly have done this on his own?"

"Don't put me on," Dawson laughed. "The FBI detachment working on this thing say it's the most sophisticated underground in the Western Hemisphere, the creation of an expert."

"And there sure ain't no spade experts, are there, Sergeant Dawson? Expertise is a white man's monopoly—they got a patent on it. You sure are brainwashed. Well, I got news for you: it's a spade scene! A spade scene, dig. You think because you've made a career out of kissing whitey's ass, every black man is in the same bag?"

"You're not going to bug me with name-calling. You don't look so swinging on the wrong end of this gun."

"Makes you a big man, don't it? A gun, a badge and a hunting license for niggers—issued by Mr. Charlie."

"I found out a long time ago, big-time, out there in those streets, that there are the people who get their heads whipped and the people who do the whipping and it didn't take long to figure out which I was going to be."

"You're a fuckin' hypocrite—all that shit about helping your people.

You want it both ways, to be supercop and have spades dig you, too. Well, you can't be a cop without betraying your people and you can't be with your people without betraying your badge." He hit Dawson in his soft spot, desperately hoping he could recruit him.

"And you think you're going to change the system, one man? There's no changing this system, not in our lifetime and maybe never and the only way to make it is get in the best spot you can find."

"I don't want to change this system, just get it off my back. I'm no fucking integrationist. Integrate into what? Whitey's welcome to his chrome-plated shit pile. I dig being black and the only thing I don't dig about being black is white folks messing with me."

"Who appointed you the savior of soul? What makes you more sensitive than anyone else? You think nobody else feels the way you do? You think there aren't days when I want to smash every white face I see? Or are you the only black man with a sense of outrage?"

"Use your outrage, hit back. Join us, Daws! We got cats on the force, but nobody with your in. Join us."

"On the force? You don't stop at anything, do you? And you been using the Cobras, them tracks in their arms got to be phony. How could you get kids involved in a thing like this?"

"Who am I going to get involved, you? You're scared shitless you might miss a promotion, not qualify for a pension. We're a wasted generation, dehydrated by whitey. I got to those kids before whitey did; they're the only hope we have."

"How are the things you're doing any better than whitey? How are you any better?"

"Why should I be? I'll do any damn thing to be free. Yeah, I'm Uncle Tom. There ain't a damn thing nonviolent about me. Anything whitey can do to keep me on my ass, I can do double to be free and when I'm gone there are others to take my place."

"I've heard enough! Let's go."

"Sure, man, cuff me." Freeman rose, Dawson still seated, and held his hands forward for the handcuffs.

Dawson reached for the cuffs in his back pocket and, as he did, the change of his weight in the foam rubber chair threw him off-balance for a moment and his gun barrel shifted. He saw it in Freeman's eyes even before he began the kick, and with the way of an athlete Dawson compensated for his imbalance: even as he moved further into the enveloping softness of the chair, he brought his gun up and fired without aiming. Freeman's kick sent Dawson over backward with the chair, the gun spinning away, but the shot had hit Freeman a glancing blow in the side, half spinning him. Noticing that Freeman had been hit, Dawson moved for the weapon on all fours, but Freeman, recovering, kicked him again in the side, sending the gun slithering across the room on the nylon carpeting. Dawson turned on his knees toward Freeman with his arms crossed in front of his face in a judo defense, ready to block, parry, or grasp a flailing leg; groggy, but still dangerous. Freeman faked a kick and when Dawson covered, chopped him hard on the junction of the neck with the edge of his hand. Dawson fell to all fours and another kick turned him over. Freeman, moving in, chopped him hard on either side of the neck and grasping his collar with either hand, one crossed over the other, he applied pressure until the muscles of his arms ached from the strain. He released him and knew before he searched for a pulse that Dawson was dead.

He squatted at the side of his dead companion, rocking back and forth on his heels. "Shit, Daws, shit. Why you, man, why did it have to be you? Anybody else, anybody."

Abruptly he stood and when he looked at the dead body of his friend, his face was impassive, except for one fleeting moment. He walked to the phone and dialed.

"Daddy? This is Turk. You get that stuff moved? Good. Get out to my place right away, it's Condition Red. And bring one of the big mail sacks. I got something for you to move."

He walked to the bathroom and stripped to the waist to check the wound. It did not look good and was bleeding freely. He dusted it with sulfa powder, placed a gauze compress against it and a thick towel over that. Returning to the bedroom he put on a loose sports shirt and a cardigan. He checked himself in the mirror and there was no telltale bulge. He walked to the living room and put a stack of records on the stereo and mixed a stiff drink. Then he sat down in the dark room to await the arrival of his lieutenants.

Dawson was too good a cop not to report where he was going, or check in when he could. When they found his body, Freeman's cover would be blown and probably that of the Cobras as well. The pain began to eat into him and he thought that his cover might not matter anyway. A doctor would have to treat him and there would be no first-class surgical facilities they could use if necessary. They would all have to go underground now. At least he wouldn't have to kill Joy to protect the cover.

He called a doctor he had recruited and told him to come by a half hour before curfew. The doorbell rang and he opened it to let in Daddy, Scott, Stud and Pretty Willie. He motioned to the bedroom.

"In the bedroom. Take it out and dump it somewhere."

"It's Dawson!" said Dean. They crowded around the body.

"Not Dawson?" said Stud. "He's your main man, how could you kill Dawson? It would be like me killing Daddy."

"And maybe one day you'll have to kill Daddy, or Daddy you. Yeah, I killed him because he got in the way; anybody who gets in the way has to go—nobody counts until we're free.

"Did you think we were playing games? Killing people we don't know and don't dig? Forty percent of those paratroopers out there are black; it's a badge of honor for a black man to wear those wings. They soldier and fight to earn what no man can earn: freedom.

"Dawson's one dead black generation and you might be another, but at least you won't be dying an inch at a time. No more of whitey's con man's integration games, freedom on the installment plan, interest collected daily. Freedom now! No more begging, pleading and silent suffering.

"Don't tell me who I killed or what it cost to do it; if you can't pay the dues, then get out." He paused, gazing at Dawson's body. They watched him in silence. He looked up abruptly, searching their faces in turn; he nodded in satisfaction.

"Condition Red. All attack teams in the field nationwide. Hit them everywhere you can, everywhere they're fat, smug and complacent; use his strength and cockiness. Hit him, disappear and hit him again. Hound, harass, fuck with his mind. Keep gettin' up and don't back down.

"Willie, I want you to take over the D.C. operation as soon as you can get there. Here's a phone number in Washington; call her, take her out and buy her a drink for me; she drinks Johnny Walker black label.

"All right, move out." He motioned to the body. "And take that with you." They stuffed Dawson's body in the mail sack and without a word, left the apartment, their thoughts on the fighting ahead.

They're not boys anymore, Freeman thought, staring at the door of the apartment after they had left. They don't need me anymore. You grow up fast in the ghetto and I helped them grow faster than most. I wonder how many of them will be alive or free this time next year?

He poured himself a stiff drink and thought that the doctor wouldn't be of much help. Hours later he sat in the darkened living room listening to the first of the shooting, the rapid crackle of automatic weapons, the spit of rifles, the explosion of grenades. The firing grew in intensity, in counterpoint to the music, Lady Day singing "God Bless the Child."

He sipped his drink and listened. "Say it, baby," he said aloud, "sing it like it is: 'God bless the child that's got his own. . . .' Go on, you black-ass Cobras, go get your own."

Freeman smiled and the pain didn't matter anymore. In fact, for the first time in many years, he hardly hurt at all.